READY POSITIONS

The Steve Kaufman Series, Book #3

Elliot Lei

West Ridge Publishing

CHAPTER ONE

A cool breeze went across the infield on this cloudy Tuesday but not enough for any wind to pick up the dirt as had happened in the earlier innings. Steve Kaufman sat in his usual spot on the first row of the metal bleachers on the first base side of the well-manicured field where a Westfield Little League game was in progress. His chin was buried in one hand as he looked at the back of his grandson's uniform, sitting on the bench waiting for his third turn at bat.

Although his team was ahead, Steve would cringe as Noel, number 9 on the Yankees (sponsored by Free Breeze Car Wash), would soon be in the hole, then on deck, then at bat. His grandson was, to be blunt, not good, striking out his last two times with one hit after six games, a dribbler down the third base line, which one could argue was really an error by a slow third baseman. He could throw and catch okay for an eight-year-old, covering his mitt with his other hand on a fairly long throw, but his hitting skills and maybe coordination were just not there. What skills he had were enough for T-ball, but not now.

It hadn't helped that his worthless dick of a father, Shelly, had abandoned his family and Steve's daughter, Lori, at forty-one, leaving her with her daughter Stephanie, who was ten, and Noel. Piece of shit. Had to go out to Washington state to 'find himself'. An insurance salesman who couldn't sell a terrorist a discounted

AK47, spending most of his workday at bars or video poker parlors. What was Lori supposed to do now, find someone else with two young kids in tow? At least his support payments had finally arrived on time, mostly. But Lori's housewife soccer-mom days were over, and she had to go back to teaching, leaving less time for her kids. That's why Steve made every game, every recital or event for these kids that he could.

Noel was on deck now and Steve perked up, nervously rubbing his hands together.

There were runners on first and second but two outs when he stepped to the plate. Gordy Graff, Noel's coach, yelled, "Come on Noel, be a hitter!" which was usually what you said to players who weren't. Noel swung at the first pitch, which was a bit outside, but he actually made contact with the ball. It arched over the second baseman, but the right fielder was playing shallow and charged the ball, making a diving catch. Cheers from the crowd. Inning over.

When the game ended, Noel wandered over to Steve, who took off his grandson's cap and tousled his hair. "Hi Papa, did you see that catch I made, the foul ball behind first base?"

It was pretty routine, but he praised the boy. "I did. Nice one. It ended the inning." Nothing was said about the hitting part of things. "Is mom getting you? She didn't say anything when she texted you had a game."

"Yeah, she'll be by in a few."

"Hey Mr. Kaufman, how you doing?" asked Gordy Graff.

"Good, Gordy, how are your folks?" Steve knew his parents from the bank.

"Great. They just got back from Florida last month. Ran into Barry down there a couple times." Barry is Steve's son, forty-five, a former lawyer and now a commodities trader for the last twelve years, named after Steve's famous Grandma Bess.

"Probably saw him more than I do," Steve replied. They both laughed. "Tell them I said hi."

"I will, take care." Just once he'd like to hear the coach say 'Good game' to Noel, but today was not that day.

His daughter Lori pulled up in her Nissan SUV with that screeching sound from the front wheel he'd heard before. She got out with her blue rain slicker on, the middle three buttons buttoned but not the top or bottom two, old sweatpants and her blond hair in a short ponytail starting to come undone. From a distance of fifteen or twenty feet, she looked like her late mother Becky.

"When are you going to get that front wheel looked at for the tenth damned time?"

"Daddy, stop. I need to find a time after school, and don't swear in front of Noel."

"Then let me take it in one day and you'll use my Lincoln."

"I'm not using your precious car; I'd be scared to get any fingermarks on it. How'd
  Noel do?"

"I made a big catch to end an inning," the boy said.

Steve looked at Lori with concern. "Wasn't your neighbor, Brian, going to practice hitting with him?"

"He's supposed to, but he's been busy."

"Forget him. I'm talking to your brother. He taught his kids; he can spend an hour or two with his nephew. If I wasn't riddled with arthritis in my back, I'd do it myself."

"You really don't need to drag Barry into this dad, he'll just resent it and..."

3

"No, he won't. And he can help you out once in a while."

"He has his own kids to raise, or are you forgetting that?"

"Look Lori, he played baseball in high school *and* college. Both his sons are star athletes, particularly in baseball. They're doing just fine, but now his nephew needs help. Done, case closed. I gotta run."

"Fine. What about that lady from Highland Park we were going to talk about? You said you'd consider it."

"Well, I haven't yet. Talk to you later." He didn't want to see the look of disgust on her face, so he yelled, "Bye Noel, remember about the show. Any night but Wednesday. And any movie but robots." He wheeled around and headed for his car.

Steve put the Lincoln Navigator in gear. He always smiled when he did because it had push button drive on the dashboard, last seen in his dad's Chrysler Imperial when he was growing up in West Ridge on the North Side of Chicago. He was trying to remember if he took a skirt steak out of the freezer and put it in the fridge earlier in the day as he drove from the Westfield Park District ball field off of Techny Road to his home in the Stone Creek Subdivision, a forty plus year old small subdivision of fifty single-story patio homes in the sleepy suburb.

One main north-south road, Remini Drive, ran through Stone Creek, with the homes on five short streets, each ending in a cul-de-sac, with ten homes on each street, each street on the east side of Remini made up the subdivision. He liked to remember the five streets in order as a sort of memory test: Fox, Powell, Easy, Aronson, and Winship, with Steve living at 191 Powell. On the west side of Remini was a forest preserve and the western boundary of the suburb. Beyond that, the Tri State Tollway. All the homes were very similar in layout, with two bedrooms and an office or study, with basements and two-car garages.

He pulled into the garage with Darius Rucker just finishing *All Right*. He was always in high spirits when he heard that song. Steve disengaged the alarm on the panel by the garage door. The most valuable item there was his full set of Titleist clubs and in the house itself probably his guns and some vintage watches. He peered into the fridge with a sigh of relief as the skirt steak had been put in to defrost so he could grill. He then looked at the calendar from a realtor on the side of the fridge and next to today's date, June 4th, 2024. He had penned in a number which he did each day, today's number being 358, meaning Becky Dean Kaufman had died 358 days ago.

He sighed and thought of her, how she battled cancer back in 1981 against long odds and beat it. Called herself a survivor. And then forty-two years later it came back, quickly and suddenly, and then she wasn't. They were supposed to grow old together, get a second place together. She had even wanted to take up golf and Steve, with his lanky frame, good drive and an eight handicap, was so happy to teach her. But he never got the chance.

And now he was alone. Oh sure, the kids and the grandkids came around lots of times those first few months, trying to include him in everything they did, but then they didn't. Most of his friends were married except for The Big Three, as he called them. They asked him to join their group, which met on Wednesday nights as they all lived in Stone Creek.

There was Stu Green, his retired accountant, and another cancer widower. There was also Al Diamond, a retiree who had owned a restaurant supply company, his wife passing many years ago, and Mike Baricello, an ex-Chicago detective cop who now did desk work for the Westfield Police Department. Still working, he claimed, because his ex-wife had cleaned him out. There had been another member, Jack Heller, a criminal lawyer of some note, but he had missed so many Wednesdays from being out of town or working late that they finally asked him to consider leaving, which he did.

This was Steve's highlight of the week. The married friends asked him to go out with them on the first few Saturday nights, but one could see there was a lot of 'couples talk' and it became awkward. Even though he had prepared himself for the future, he really hadn't. He thought with golf, shooting, maybe even taking up fishing again after so many years, that his time would be filled. But even if he went say golfing on Sundays for the regular game at Ivanhoe, when it was done, his foursome would say see you next week and go home to their spouses and he was left alone again, sometimes indefinitely. God, he missed her.

So every Wednesday, the Big Three ordered in or picked up dinner and watched sports on TV at Stu's house. No one wanted or really could cook, and Steve did enjoy it as they talked about everything and they were all bright, Mike included, being a former homicide detective and serving on a couple of joint federal task forces. This, however, was Tuesday and the skirt steak from his Weber grill on the small patio in back, plus a baked potato and some Trader Joe's coleslaw would have to suffice. He always noticed that since she was gone, it took him about an hour to make dinner, twenty minutes to eat it, then another half hour to clean up.

God, he missed her cooking. In their old house near downtown Westfield, she had a spice rack with items he didn't even know existed and a huge pantry. Even when she was sick, she still cooked until she couldn't, said it made her feel better, feel useful. He had asked Stu and Al if he would ever get over missing her so much, when almost every other thought of his had her come to mind. "It will get a bit better," they said, "but no, not ever."

After dinner, he went into his study and leaned back in his desk chair and sighed. As he flipped open his laptop to Google something on-line, he thought of tomorrow when he would go to Gat Guns gun range in East Dundee for target practice, taking his two guns, a Smith & Wesson EZ 9-millimeter semi-automatic and his revolver, a Smith & Wesson model 686-6 .357 magnum revolver, which he had purchased as a gift for himself at the end of last year.

He had never really been into guns until a long-time close friend, Greg Orlov, had introduced them to him about two years ago, telling him it was a fun sport and a great way to relieve stress. He scoffed at first, but went to a couple of ranges with Greg and fell in love with the sport. Greg had probably six guns, and they went to local ranges, sometimes three times a week. But that all ended. Greg had a winter place in Florida in Fort Lauderdale and never came back north, being killed by a drunk driver in Miami, who hit him head on.

Steve was obviously devastated but would still go to the ranges once in a while, something else to do alone now, although it wasn't the same. He looked around the room, swiveled his chair around to the built-in bookshelves behind him to see the family photos going back some forty years. His gaze swept over the photos of the family, photos with celebrities and golfing buddies. Then it settled on his father's framed medals from the Korean War, including the Purple Heart and a Bronze Star for valor at the Chosin Reservoir. Beside the medals were the awards and certificates of appreciation for all the civic work he and Becky had done.

All right, he thought, push that stuff aside and get to why you came in here, to Google your son and find if there were any stories on-line about a Board of Trade commodities scandal that had the feds looking into people for insider trading and committing fraud. Thankfully, finding nothing, although there were articles on two other traders he knew of, he shut his laptop down and went into his bedroom to watch a movie on Netflix. The phone would not ring that night, nor would he have called anyone, a typical night.

That night at about eleven o'clock four streets over on Winship Drive, a black Mercedes pulls into a driveway and before the driver opens the garage door, he fumbles for some paperwork in his center console. His front door is suddenly pulled open from the outside by someone with a red hoodie and jeans and he is shot four times with a Glock 19. With the door still open and the engine running, the driver is bent over, his legs and torso still in his car seat while his head and shoulders lay on the driveway pavement.

CHAPTER TWO

Stu calls Steve on his way back from Gat Guns late Wednesday morning. "The boys called. Two things. First, did you hear about Jack Heller? It's all over the news."

"No, I left early this morning. What's up?"

"He was murdered last night in his driveway. Neighbor heard shots and called the cops. They found him dead, half in his seat and half on the pavement, motor in the car still running."

"No shit! Wow, Jack? I can't believe that. I just saw him over the weekend at the gas station."

"I can't believe you didn't hear about it. On the radio and TV news and everything. There hasn't been a murder in this town in at least ten years."

"Well," Steve sighs, "it'll make for some interesting conversation, as they say tonight, I'm sure."

"That's the second thing," Stu replies. "Mike is gonna be in Vernon Hills on his way home from a police conference in Libertyville and wants to stop off at Urban Barbecue in Lincolnshire or Vernon Hills, wherever the heck it is. Al and I are in. What would you want?"

"Well, it's good I've got a voice in this. A half slab of St. Louis ribs with slaw."

"Okay, that's what I'm getting. Hey, remember the days we could eat a full slab?"

"Yeah, fifty some years ago maybe," Steve says a bit wistfully. "See you at six."

Steve was in a semi-trance. How could Jack Heller be dead? He remembers briefly talking to him at the BP gas station on Sunday. It was brief because every conversation with Jack was brief. He was always in a hurry, and Sunday was no exception.

He had said, "Hi, how's it going?" But he didn't ask about anything else except he went into a brief rant about the price of gas and how he wished he had a car that took regular instead of 'this gas guzzling overpriced German piece of shit.'

"Fair enough," Steve had said. And then he was gone, hopped back into his car and sped off. And now he was gone forever. Steve had often wondered about that. You're with somebody, whether it be a spouse, parents, a friend, Jack Heller, one day and then it turns out that's the last time you see them. Even with Becky when she was at home in hospice and Lori was by her bedside, Steve ran to the drug store and when he returned, she was gone. How do you ever get used to that?

His dad would tell him stories about his time as a medic in Korea when he had to make choices on a battlefield as to how to treat the wounded. Steve had asked him that it seemed obvious you would treat the most serious wounds first, but his dad shook his head. "No Stevie, you got to know by instinct and with limited medical supplies and the cold who to treat first. You treated the guys who you thought had a chance of surviving, not the ones you knew didn't have a chance. All you could do for them was maybe relieve the suffering." It seemed so matter of fact, but he said by the time he himself was wounded in the butt and sent home, he then realized how crazy it all was.

He pulls up the driveway and grabs his mail out of the

mailbox before going into the garage. An electric bill and four solicitations for charities. He had not given many donations since she'd been gone. It was almost like he was punishing the charities for her death, although he knew that was insane.

The house is quiet except for the Seth Thomas clock on the fireplace mantel with its soothing tick that would help him to sleep many a night while reading in his Eames lounge chair. He changed into a tracksuit and his Hokas, turns his head under the kitchen faucet for a drink (something he used to do when Becky wasn't looking) and goes out the front door for a run. But his mind keeps going back to Jack Heller. He had represented lots of Outfit guys before slowing down his practice, with considerable success, but hell, it just takes one guy he didn't get off or who wasn't happy to order a hit. Wait, do they still have mob hits? Then there was the messy divorce with Sheila that had just finished. But even if she hated his guts, what good was he to her dead? Insurance? Well, it'll certainly be the topic of discussion later.

He reaches Lake Cook Road and continues jogging by the forest preserve, but he feels tired already. Not necessarily out of breath or winded, but just tired. Turning around, he is reminded of a physical he has coming in a few weeks on a Thursday afternoon with blood tests earlier in the week. Entering the house, he looks at his watch and decides to take a nap, then shower and get ready for the boys.

CHAPTER THREE

He throws on an open tail button-down shirt and pair of jeans, sets the alarm, then lopes the two houses down to Stu Green's house. Stu had been his friend and accountant for thirty years and that was the reason he lived in the Stone Creek Subdivision. When Stu lost his wife, Anne, several years ago, he had moved to this house from his colonial near downtown Westfield. His three kids were gone. It was much too big and there were too many memories. The exact same scenario followed Steve; except he had two kids rather than three. And the house two doors down from Stu's new place just happened to have a widower named Howard Lake whose family needed him to move into an assisted living facility in Deerfield after falling repeatedly, the last time resulting in serious injury.

He could see Al Diamond's Lexus SUV and Mike Baricello's Jeep in Stu's driveway, even though it wasn't quite six o'clock. He didn't knock or ring a bell, just turned the front door handle. They were all at the kitchen table, unwrapping the food.

"Oh my God," Steve said. "You guys are like vultures. Like you're seeing food for the first time."

"We're hungry," Baricello snaps. "I had a roll and a bad cup of coffee at that conference this morning. That's it."

"Yeah? Well, what's their excuse?" Steve replies.

"We're just making sure Mike gets it right, divides it up okay," Stu says, pointing a finger up to make a point. "You want a beer or two kinds of diet pop?"

"None of the above. You have just ice water?"

"Take a look inside the fridge. There's a row of bottles in there."

The ribs were good and even though Steve wasn't starving like Al and Mike seemed to be, he kept pace with everyone, even Mike, who never seemed to eat food but attacked it. There was very little discourse at dinner, just chewing, grunting and occasional lip smacking or finger licking of at least three different kinds of barbeque sauces. When the boxes and paper plates are cleared, Stu announces he has gelato bars and Keto sugar free ice cream in two different flavors. Everyone except Mike goes for the Keto cartons as everyone, including Mike, has type two diabetes. After polishing off the ice cream, everyone assembles in the living room as Stu turns on the Cubs game just about to start on his absurdly large screen TV.

"Oh damn," says Al. "Isn't there anything else on? They suck. The great underachievers!"

"What, we should watch your Sox? The worst team in baseball?" Stu shoots back.

"Can you even get the Sox on TV anymore?" Mike adds.

"I get like a thousand channels," Stu sort of sniffs. "I can get minor league soccer from Djibouti."

"Put on whatever," Al waives a hand at Stu in disgust. "Let's talk about Jack Heller."

"True. Why don't you mute it Stu," Steve answers. "Mike, what do you know about the case?"

Mike folds his arms and clears his throat in an authoritative way. The officer of the law, the expert. "Well, the boys at the Westfield main station where I'm at are rubbing their hands together. Don't forget, it's been years since they worked a murder case. Anyway, the neighbor witness, Mrs. Krause, who lives almost across the street, said she heard shots and looked out the window to see a man in a red hoodie running down the sidewalk to a car she thought was yellow and speed away. And that's all she saw, no make, model, or plate number.

"Doesn't his son Nathan have a yellow car, like a Camaro or Charger, some sports coupe?" asks Stu.

"Yes, I've seen it," Al says as Mike nods in agreement.

"It's hard to miss," says Steve. "Where does he live now, with Sheila?"

"Yep. She's got a condo apartment near the Edens in Highland Park off of Lake Cook
Road. They're gonna question both of them and then look at former clients, any disgruntled Outfit guys," Mike adds. "There is no funeral, no service even. That's what he wanted. He's being cremated once the coroner releases the body. "

"That's gotta be a long list of suspects," Al shakes his head.

"What about the gun?" Steve asks Mike.

"A Glock 19. Found three shell casings. This was no random shooting."

"That's a pretty common handgun, lots of them out there," Steve replies.

"You would know." Stu looked at Steve sarcastically. He could never understand why he was into guns.

Steve ignores the comment and looks at Mike. "Any other evidence they find?"

"Na, just checking for footprints on the grass on the lawns

down the street where whoever it was ran, fingerprints on the car or by the house and the house itself."

"Hey, we should go over there and poke around. I mean, it's still light out," says Al.

"Come on Al, be real. What do you know about what to even look for? In any case, they'll be out there in the morning, and I asked to go along so we'll see everything then and go in the house to see if there are any clues there." This is Mike exercising his authority.

"But why can't we all go now?" Al replies.

"It would be cool," Steve nods. "You could tell us what to look for."

Mike scoffs. "Steve, I haven't done this in years. *I'm* not sure what to look for. And we could be messing up a crime scene."

"Mike, what you did on the force can't have changed that much and we wouldn't be touching anything," Al said, short of saying, oh pretty please.

Mike sighs and looks at Stu, sort of the de facto head of the group. "Stu, it's your call."

"Like Al said, while it's still light out."

They climb into Mike's Jeep and drive the four streets down to Winship Lane. The house and driveway are taped off with that yellow and black crime scene tape with the familiar number tags on the ground where the shell casings were found like one sees on TV. They don't cross the tape but do walk down the street in the direction of where the killer would have run to the car. It was Stu who found it.

"Look, a wrapper for Trident Gum." He points by the street gutter about two houses down.

Mike runs up. "Don't touch it!" He reaches in his pocket for an evidence bag, then he also retrieves a pair of latex gloves from another pocket, placing the gum wrapper in the bag. "We'll run it in the morning for prints in the lab. Not much of a clue, but you never know."

Further down the street, Al yells, "There's tire marks here or parts of them."

Everyone jogs down the street and stands where Al is pointing. The light was starting to fade and Stu and Steve turn on the flashlights on their phones.

"Do you think they could match these with Nathan's car?" Stu asks Mike.

"Could be. I'll point it out to the crew in the morning," Mike answers. "They look pretty fresh."

As they walk back to the Jeep, there is a look of satisfaction from everyone except Mike.

"That was so cool," Al says.

"Wow," Steve adds.

"It is a murder, you realize," Stu replies.

"Yeah, but to think that maybe we're helping to solve it and..."

"Whoa," Mike cuts Al short. "This is an awfully long way from being solved. And if any of it applies, it's all circumstantial."

Back at Stu's house, they continue to ponder the scene and the possibilities, believing that the suspects so far were Nathan, possibly but not likely Sheila, and some former client of Jack Heller's. They went on to talk about restaurants opening and closing, a new health club opening up and the ineptness of the Village Board of Westfield in turning down a new Walgreens within walking distance of Stone Creek because Walgreens wanted a drive through pharmacy lane, something the Village had never approved.

By ten o'clock they were all yawning. When you're in your seventies the days are shorter, even in the summer. Mike says he would call Stu about any developments in the Heller case and Stu would pass it on, as things might move quickly before they met next Wednesday. Everyone realizes Mike was actually violating the law by disclosing information to outsiders about a pending case, but they all knew nothing they discussed would ever leave Stu's house.

As Steve enters the house, his phone rings.

"Hi Daddy, you in the house?" Lori asks.

"Yes honey, just walked in. What's up?"

"Did you talk to Barry yet?"

"Not yet, but we're meeting Friday morning for breakfast."

"Okay, Noel has a game Saturday, but I'm calling for another reason."

Steve tensed up; he knew what was coming. "And what's that?"

"My girlfriend's mom, Candace Miller, the Highland Park woman I've been trying to talk to you about forever."

"I've never heard of someone named Candace. Now Candy, that's different. I knew a Candy in high school and down at Illinois and come to think of it at graduate school at Northwestern, there was a Candy in a couple of my classes. But Candace, no, that makes no sense."

"Dad, stop. What difference does it make? You're just being difficult. She's a very nice woman, your age, fairly good looking, and she's active. Oh, and blond hair. I know you like blond hair."

"Honey, at my age, no one's really blond. Okay, is she a

widow, divorced? What's the deal? You're going to hound me about this until I call her or drop dead."

"She's divorced, for a few years now, but her ex passed away recently, so I guess both."

"So, you're saying we have something in common? Have you met her? What's she like?"

Lori sighed. "Yes, several times, she's my good friend Linda Miller's mom. You've met Linda. She likes you, thinks you're a sweet guy. She is also a great therapist. I've told you Daddy, you should see her professionally. You can relate to her and she to you."

"Yes, I have met Linda. And I've told you, when you find me a therapist who is in his or her seventies and lost a spouse, *that* person maybe I can relate to. And she's not blond. She's the tennis player friend of yours, right? Her mom play?"

"Yes, I think she does. See, she's in shape. So can I give you her number? She's expecting a call."

Now he sighs, giving up. "All right already, tomorrow night I'll call."

After giving him the number, she says, "Oh and Dad, please don't mention that you own guns and shoot."

"Oh, for God's sake Lori, that's going to come out sooner or later, if there is a later."

"Just for now, please?"

"Just for now. It's late. I trust everything else is okay?" Why was it so exhausting to talk to my daughter is all he could think.

"Yes, thank you Dad. Maybe if this works out, you'll be thanking me."

"Or not. Night Lori."

"Night Daddy."

CHAPTER FOUR

Thursday morning Steve goes to the health club for a swim and then to the barber to see Cecelia who has been cutting his hair for fifteen years. He would rib her because their prices had gone up through the years but in his case, she had less hair to cut. But she always gave him a discount because nine years ago her father, a mechanic down in Pilsen, had always wanted to open up his own shop in the Mexican neighborhood. Financing, however, was going to prove difficult to buy the small garage building he wanted and get all the equipment and tools. Steve handled large real estate loans, but he managed to refer him to a banker at a branch down there who set him up. Cecelia had never forgotten that.

Thursdays were always hard for Steve. Once he had retired from the bank, he would join Becky to grocery shop which she did every Thursday for many years. They would drive the few blocks to Sunset Foods, and she would go through each aisle methodically filling their grocery cart from her list while he wandered around the store like a five year old finding stuff like mango ice cream bars and Australian black licorice, things he liked but that no one needed. A smile would still come to him when he thought about it and before he realized it, his eyes were wet.

Now on Thursdays he was at the Golf Tech driving range in

Des Plaines hitting a bucket of balls or he'd find a show to go to, anything to take his mind off the fact that it was Thursday. By the time he got back home, even though it was only about three thirty, he felt exhausted. He took a nap but didn't set an alarm and two hours later he woke up, just in time for the five-thirty national news. After looking at some unappetizing grilled chicken pieces in the fridge, he decided he had a taste for a roast beef sandwich at Subway so off he went.

As soon as he got back to the house the phone rang. It was Stu.

"Hey what's up?" Stu asks.

"Nada. Had a taste for Subway so I went out for a bit. You?"

"The kids both stopped by. They brought in ribs," Stu laughed.

"Ha! Were you hungry for em' after last night?" Steve laughs as well, but he is envious. He couldn't remember the last time one of his kids brought dinner over let alone both of them.

"You know, I was. And I had chicken. They stopped by that chicken and rib joint in Wilmette on Lake Street. Anyway, Mike called a bit ago right before dinner. Said they went back to Heller's place, searched the house and took his computer and phone to check. They also made a mold or some kind of cast of that tire mark and Mike said the results came back already. Get this, the tire is a General G-Max AS-7, high performance twenty-inch tires which are on 2023 Dodge Chargers."

"Doesn't that match to the yellow car Nathan has, a Charger?"

"No, that's just it. Steve, his car is yellow but it's a Camaro," Stu replied. "They believe the Camaro has Goodyear tires and might be nineteen inches, not twenty but they won't know for sure until they check out Nathan's car. They're interviewing

Nathan and Sheila tomorrow."

"Wow. Is Mike going along?"

"Oh yeah, and he's loving it. Not being behind the desk but out in the field again. You sound tired."

"I am, even though I came home from the driving range at three thirty and took a two-hour nap. You know I have that blood test and physical in about ten days."

"Well, I hope you're okay. Listen, I gotta call Al and tell him what's going on before he goes out to a play which his granddaughter's in. I'll talk to ya."

"Sounds good Stu."

Steve looks at his watch, almost seven thirty. He'd better call Candace before it was any later. He takes the number from the paper on his desk in the office and dials, nervously rocking back and forth in his swivel chair. He remembers she was divorced for a while and then her husband died from melanoma, if that ever came up.

"Hello?" She sounded cheerful.

"Hi, is this Candace?"

"Yes, who's this?"

"Hi Candace. This is Steve Kaufman, Lori Kaufman's dad. How are you?" Boy that sounded dumb.

"I'm fine Steve, how are you doing?" Again, cheerful, maybe too much so. Stop it! Move on.

"I'm well, thank you. My daughter thought and err, well, I thought too that we might get together."

"Well, that would be lovely, Steve. What did you have in mind?" This woman could deliver flowers to a funeral.

"I was wondering if you were free Saturday night, or Sunday for brunch, um, or dinner." I'm kind of open," he laughed mildly thinking what an idiot, you sound lonely and desperate.

"Saturday night is fine. Did you have anywhere in mind?" Again, it was like talking to Doris Day.

"Um, would Italian be okay? I was thinking of Emilio's in Deerfield, it's not too noisy and the food's always good."

"Sure. Nice place. Would you pick me up or?"

"Oh, of course, unless you wanted to meet me there, I mean you don't know me yet and, I'm sorry, you gotta forgive me, I haven't asked someone out or gone on a date in like over forty years and I'm truly out of practice." Now he really sounded desperate as the chair was rocking back and forth.

She laughs again, "Don't worry, you're doing fine. Just fine. How's six thirty, I'll text you my address, it's a condo building on Second Street south of downtown Highland Park."

"Oh, okay. That would be great. And thanks for, well, making this easy, easier I should say, for me."

She laughs again. "Not a problem. I'll be downstairs in front of my building."

"I'm looking forward to it. See you then."

"As I am, bye."

"Yes, bye."

The last time he remembered heaving a sigh of relief like this was after he asked Rebecca Dean to marry him, and she had said yes.

He settled in to watch a Jason Statham movie on cable when the phone rang at about nine thirty. Lori. Oh shit. She's going to want to know if I called, if so' how did it go? Ad nauseum.

"Hi Daddy."

"What's up honey?" Statham was just finishing up beating the crap out of like a dozen guys at once, so he paused the film, very disappointed to do so.

"Well two things. I wanted to let you know about Noel's game on Saturday at nine thirty by one of the fields at Village Green, if you wanted to go. And second, I just talked to Linda Miller who talked to her mother earlier. Her mother thought you were adorable."

"I just talked to her like two hours ago, does the whole town know? And adorable, what does that mean?"

"It means nice Dad, better than nice. You did great, I know it couldn't have been easy. Like thirty some years ago for you."

"Try forty-some. And yes, I'll be there. Did you check your car yet?"

"I am tomorrow; my neighbor's brother is a mechanic at a place on Waukegan Road.
Oh, I have to run, Stephanie and Noel are fighting again about something."

"Okay, bye."

CHAPTER FIVE

Stuart Green sat in his bathrobe on his bed thumbing through a plastic-covered notebook with a diary/journal he was keeping. About six months ago he had been very depressed. Anne was gone for four years now, and they had done everything together, they finished each other's thoughts as he'd like to say. They had no children but were incredibly happy. She was a successful psychologist, he was a partner in a national CPA firm but had many local clients like Steve Kaufman, and they busied themselves with an active social life and constant travel.

But when you're alone after a while friends who are married or widowed and then dating again call less and less and add that to the fact that his only outside activity was golf and an occasional dip in the health club pool, he had little to do. Thank goodness for the Wednesday night group and his breakfast group of retired accountants every other Saturday morning. Then there were the nieces and nephews and grand nieces and nephews as Anne had four brothers and sisters, and he had two brothers. Otherwise, his phone would hardly ring.

Friends of theirs had tried to fix him up on dates but he never clicked with anyone, admittedly because he compared them all to Anne. So out of the blue one day after going for a walk in the rain and oblivious to the fact that he was soaked, he went through an old Rolodex and found her number, Beth Kirvitsky. She was a psychologist who had worked with Anne years ago and they had remained close. As he explained to her, he was depressed and felt like he was losing his mind and possibly thought about harming himself.

He had seen her now for three months at her office in Park Ridge. One of her 'coping exercises' was for him to start the journal.

"What would I write in it?" he shrugged. "I don't really do anything."

"Write whatever comes to mind," she replied. "Then look at it later and remember how you felt when you wrote that down."

He had doubts but that all changed two months ago. There was a spot of dead grass behind his home. They were called patio homes because they had what's known as zero lot lines in front and only a small area in back where there was a patio. All the landscaping, front and back and in between the houses was maintained by the Stone Creek Homeowners Association. For over a year now Stuart had put in a request to replace the dead grass that was almost four feet in diameter that abutted his patio. His frustration seemed to grow daily, and he finally decided he would do it himself. How damned difficult could it be? Dig out the dead grass, put in some topsoil and lay a couple of pieces of sod over it after cutting it into shape. He still had garden tools in the garage from the old house. Yes, his back would curse him but on a sunny Saturday in late April he set out for a landscaping company on Skokie Boulevard just south of Dundee.

After talking to Rick at DiFiori's Landscaping Company and explaining what he wanted to do, the young college student from Dayton showed him the two bags of top soil and pieces of sod. It was ryegrass to match what was there and asked if he needed any digging tools. Stuart had his dad's army shovel from the Second World War, so he was set. After piling everything in his Toyota SUV he spotted a Starbucks just down the street and thought it might be time for a latte.

There was one woman ahead of him in line and after ordering she turned around and smiled at him and he smiled back. She was Asian, late fifties or early sixties, her long hair pulled back and tied with a red bow and a purple sweater with a small purple and white "N" by her chest. A Northwestern Wildcat. He should know. He did his undergrad work there before going to Illinois for his CPA.

He waited at the pickup line behind her, and she headed for the end of two double square tables, one of the last seats in this small store, after the barista called out her name, "Anne." Stuart half gasped. How wild is that?

He took a seat at the other end of the double tables. He noticed that he and Anne were the only ones not staring at their phones or tablets. She seemed to be staring off in the distance, as if either daydreaming or contemplating something. It would be rude to interrupt her but in the split second that he checked the time on his watch she turned to him and smiled.

"Nice watch," she pointed. "What make is that?"

"Oh, thanks." He felt himself blushing. "It's an Audemars Piguet. A client gave it to me as a gift."

"Are you a lawyer or..."

"Accountant. And I believe I went to school where you did." Now he pointed. "Although it was probably many years before you did."

She laughed and waved him over and they talked for over an hour. Her name was
Ann (no 'e') Chen and she was a sixty-one-year-old dentist with a solo practice in Glenview. She lived in a townhome in Wilmette, was a widow and was thirteen years his junior. They both liked classical music *and* classic rock, and she golfed! She said her

favorite restaurant was in Greek town and so they made a date for the following Saturday night at The Greek Isles.

When he got back to the car, he shook his head thinking that he had struck gold. For the first time in four years, he believed God's light had shined upon him and he felt genuinely happy. And that night the journal started. Just as the doctor ordered. But the entries, which would continue every day for the next two months, as they went everywhere although never close to home, were not about his depression or his wife or someone's kids or grandkids or the weather. They were only about Ann.

The only person who knew about them was his therapist. He wasn't even going to tell her, but his depression had lifted somewhat, and she needed to know the reason why, otherwise the therapy wouldn't be honest. The problem, of course, was as soon as he told her she, in turn, wanted to know why he didn't want his family or friends to know. He explained that because she was thirteen years younger, Asian and pretty whereas he felt he was balding, short and not good looking, that they wouldn't understand, they would be judgmental. She dismissed those notions and added that if it really was serious, wouldn't everyone find out at some point anyway? Sensing that they were going to be bogged down by this, both of them decided to let it go, at least for now.

But in their last session, they did talk about love, he actually brought it up. Of course it turned to him, what he thought it was. Was this relationship love or something else? And that led to comparisons with Anne, his wife. She asked if he kept pictures of Ann and he said he did, in the back of his journal. He had downloaded about a dozen of them from his phone and had five by seven's made at Walgreens. Pictures at The Botanic Garden, The Barn Restaurant, The Greek Isles, Roditys, The Museum of Contemporary Art, The Green Mill Jazz Club and by Northwestern at a path they walked near the lake. But again, no one knew about it except the therapist and for now, he wanted to keep it that way.

CHAPTER SIX

He tosses the Xbox aside and starts to bounce a ball against the wall of his room. If only his dad were around but Noel knew he wasn't coming back. Noel remembers so well the T-ball game where he didn't show up. He had played so well that game, two hits in three at bats and nice clean fielding at second base. He kept looking over to first base, but he wasn't there. Later, when his friend Taren's mom had dropped him off at home, he wasn't there either. Mom was in a panic and when she was ready to call the police after dinner he finally called, saying he was leaving home to go live out west in some mountain place.

Noel would see him once more when he came to collect some of his things. Mom had taken him and Stephanie to a counselor-lady she knew who explained to them that it wasn't their fault that he left, that adults often-times had things that they had to work out for themselves. But that was of little consequence to Noel or his sister. Almost immediately his friends in and out of school would talk about his dad, like who just gets up and leaves? For Stephanie it was worse because she was ten and her friends knew about divorces, and she felt like just another statistic who people whispered about behind her back. His quiet older sister whom he had always looked up to as calm and reassuring now seemed to get angry and snap about the slightest thing.

And then there was Mom. She ended up going back to work as a teacher, which she was before he and his sister were born. He had asked her why and she said it was so they could live the same type of life that they had when Dad was around. He wasn't sure exactly what that meant but knew it had something to do with money. She too used to be so calm and reassuring and was now hurried and tense. Even if they went to a show or did something fun like being at a museum, she was always looking at the time, always in a rush. He liked the old days when Dad was around, but Dad was gone.

He continues bouncing the ball and catching it, but he knows catching wasn't his problem. It was hitting. In practice the coach would pair them up and they'd throw grounders and fly balls to each other. He was always okay with that. Coach Graff would usually pair him up with his best friend Taren, taller than Noel with bangs in his eyes and a natural athlete, even at eight. But Taren could hit the ball and Noel could not. The coach would throw pitches and work a bit on swings with the team, but he lobbed the balls to the batters or had them hit off of a T like they had in T-Ball. That Noel could do but if a pitcher threw overhand to him as they did in games, he seemed afraid of the ball. Mom couldn't help, all she could do was lob the ball to him too. And Mr. Weston down the block, who mom asked to help him hit, had to go out of town on business twice when he was supposed to come by.

He throws the ball harder at his wall, aiming for a drawing of a butterfly he did in science class learning about metamorphosis from Mrs. Scoyk, his teacher, who had been extra kind to him when she found out the family situation. He could ruin the drawing but doesn't care.

He finally stops throwing and looks at a photo on top of his chest of drawers on the side wall of his bedroom with the window on it. It is a picture of his extended family on his mom's side, taken a few years back when he was five in his grandfather's yard. He's in the front row, on the grass, next to his sister and older cousins Randy and Paul. Behind them are his mother, Uncle Barry, Aunt Michelle and his Papa Steve and Grandma Becky. Noel's dad was away on business. In the picture Noel has a puzzled look on his face but he remembers being happy. It was springtime or summer, like now, and he remembers so well when dinner was finished how they all walked down the street to a park where his cousins, uncle and even Papa Steve played baseball. Now both his cousins played baseball and were really good. Paul is on the Westfield High School Team and Randy plays in junior high. Noel knew they were very busy with their own schedules but wishes they had time for him. As his eyes moistened all he could think was that life wasn't fair.

CHAPTER SEVEN

Friday morning Steve has trouble getting out of bed. His back issues are present again and even though he had had a fusion at L 3 and 4 right after Becky died, the pain now seems to have traveled down to his lower spine. He was due to go to the surgeon right after his physical in a couple weeks. After popping a pain killer and his vitamins he gets dressed. It is a big day, as he is meeting his son Barry for breakfast at the Egg Factory. He hasn't seen him in almost a month as Barry seems to be constantly busy and was in Arizona on a golf trip with his trader buddies this past week.

What a schmuck, Steve thought. My forty-five-year-old son went from being a trial lawyer with a downtown firm to a precious metals trader and a conservative, down-to-earth guy to a big shot with cars, trips and living the high life. Added to that he hadn't called his family, meaning Steve and his sister, for literally weeks and Steve, normally an easygoing, live and let live kind of guy, was downright pissed. But Steve wasn't going to read him the riot act, just see how things were going and talk about Noel, the real reason to see him. Steve smirked. There's nothing like a parent making a child feel guilty, no matter how old they both are.

Whenever Barry seemed to be getting too big of an ego, Steve would think of the American Graveco story. Years back, some junior loan officers at the bank got wind of a new stock IPO, an unknown company that imported a supposedly revolutionary type of skin care product. "Hey Mr. Kaufman," one of the very junior loan officers said, "Have you heard about American Graveco, this new IPO that's set to hit the market next Wednesday? We're all going in on it."

"No Mike, I really haven't."

"You should check it out. It's gonna be huge. Ask your son, I bet he knows about it."

So he did. And Barry and his buddies had heard about it and were going in on it. "You should too Dad, call your broker or I can get you in on it. Just give me a check for however much you want, five grand minimum. But it has to be soon because next Wednesday the offer is going to be submitted in New York."

Steve said he'd think on it. The next day Steve had an appointment with his dentist downtown. It was in an old, small high rise building on Wabash Avenue. The building was so old it had elevator operators with gates instead of doors in front. Steve knew both the elevator operators after going to the building for over thirty years. One was Jerry, a Czech immigrant who happened to own a string of small apartment buildings. The American dream on full display. Jerry greeted him warmly. "Hey Mr. Steve, how are you? How's the family?"

"Good Jerry. And yours?"

"Great Mr. Steve. You going to Dr. Halper, yes?

"Of course."

Steve stepped in and Jerry continued. "You always tell me about interest rates and where the real estate market is headed, and I appreciate it. Today though, I have a tip for you. A new company coming out, check it out. American Graveco, is going public. I want to repay the favors."

Steve thanked him and his mind was made up. He would

pass on American Graveco. That next week on the Tuesday evening news David Muir told his viewers that FBI agents had met a plane at the LaGuardia Airport in New York and arrested three men who had converted millions of dollars into cash and were waiting to take a flight to the Caribbean. They were all senior executives, and the owners of a shell company named American Graveco. Steve brought it up once to Barry who admitted he, like many others, had been duped. They never spoke of it again. The junior loan officers at the bank said nothing about it either, except for months afterwards they were bringing in their lunches rather than eating out.

Steve climbs into his car with his back still bothering him. He swears at his Navigator. The seat adjusts twenty different ways and has a lumbar support, but he can't get comfortable. He then tells himself to stop it. Remember your poor wife in her last months when she couldn't get comfortable sitting, standing, or sleeping. How you prayed for her to get well against all odds when she first had cancer in eighty-one and it worked but now thought you couldn't pray for that a second time because your prayers were all used up. But you could at least pray for her not to be in pain, which you did repeatedly. Did it work? He'll never know.

He parks and the running board slips out from underneath the door. Thank God he had bought that luxury limited package as he steps down. He enters the restaurant which is more than half empty. He peers at his father's gold watch, a vintage A. Lange & Sohne, one of many his dad had left him and his brother Peter, although he had kept his while Peter had sold or pawned his.

It was eight thirty-five. The hostess asks him if he wants to wait or be seated, and he asks for a booth and coffee. Ordering ahead of time might seem disrespectful if you're waiting for someone but that was exactly Steve's intent. Plus, he wanted coffee.

Barry arrives five minutes later in a short sleeve

Blackhawks' Jeremy Roenick jersey and shorts. He is a bit shorter than Steve's six feet two frame but is powerfully built with dark, receding hair and piercing blue eyes, the latter an obvious gift from his mother. Steve gets up and they embrace.

"Dad, it's been a while, too long."

"I won't argue that. That jersey signed?" Steve says it as a joke, knowing Barry had probably a dozen signed athlete jerseys framed in his basement.

"Funny. No, but I did put a bid in on a Kobe Bryant rookie jersey yesterday and I'll know by two today if I'm high bidder."

"Where's that, on eBay?"

"Na, some auction house in Phoenix. Used em' before."

"Yeah, so what's new? How was your trip?" Steve could really give a shit about his jersey or his trip but he's your son. Act interested.

"Great, but we had to go either early or late to play eighteen holes. Even though it's June, it's still really hot there."

They talked about the family, mainly his kids, and what each of them was doing. In between they ordered breakfast and when it came, they seemed to wolf it down it as both were hungry. When they were almost done, Barry finally asked about Lori and her divorce.

Steve replied and saw an opening. "Shelly sends what he's supposed to send, but sometimes it's late. She'll be okay, she's just a bit frazzled right now. But it's not her I'm worried about."

Barry's eyes narrowed. "Then who?"

"Your nephew," Steve almost whispered.

"Noel? I heard he's fine in spite of everything. Did well in school this year, has friends...."

"Well, you heard wrong," Steve snapped. "Didn't Lori call you weeks ago about helping him out with baseball? It's the kid's favorite sport and he can't hit. He's miserable."

"I remember she called but honestly Dad, I can't remember what it was about."

"Yeah, well, that's what it's about. He can catch, field, and do everything but hit. Last year the ball was on a Tee, this year it's live pitches and he frankly sucks. I'd get over there myself, but if I turn the wrong way, I'm in the E.R. Room."

"No, I understand what you're saying, but I don't think I'm a hitting coach." He shakes his head.

"Barry, come on. Don't bullshit me. You played ball and you've got two sons that eat and breathe the sport. The kid's beside himself and so his mother is miserable, and that makes me miserable." He glares at Barry. "And I don't like being miserable."

Barry closes his eyes and sighs. "Okay, what if I stop by Lori's today before dinner and see what I can do? Give him a few pointers."

"That would work. Or you could ask Paul or Randy to stop by. It would do them good, performing like a mitzvah."

"No Dad," Barry shakes his head. "They're just coming home from a baseball minicamp in Maine, and I've got more time than they do anyway. As soon as they're back, they've both got summer traveling leagues."

Steve nods. He can sense Barry is uncomfortable because he's fidgeting. Steve does that as his dad did. It's a telltale sign the Kaufman men seem to have. Steve changes the subject. "Okay, done, thank you. Did you hear about Jack Heller?"

"I did. You think it was a mob hit?"

"Don't know. He was just finished with a nasty divorce."

"Aww, come on. Why would his wife, what's her name again, do anything like that?"

"Sheila."

"Yeah, that's it, Sheila. If it was for insurance money, the company wouldn't pay her a dime until she's ruled out as a suspect."

"My son, the lawyer. But you're probably right. We'll have to see what comes out."

They talk for a few minutes about Barry's uncle Peter, the Vegas wonder who has won and lost fortunes three times that Steve knows of, not in gambling but in the car dealership business, new and used.

As they walk outside, Steve sees Barry walking to a gray Mercedes GLE450 SUV.

"What happened to your Jeep Wagoneer?" Steve asks. "You were raving about that car when you got it."

"Uh, it didn't ride great and I just kinda got tired of it."

Steve rolls his eyes. "You know you're a schmuck, don't you?"

"Good seeing you too Dad."

Steve cursed himself. He didn't see his son that often and now when he did, they ended on a sour note. But then he defended himself. What was wrong with saving some money as opposed to impressing people? And okay, Steve's Lincoln was not cheap, but he got it for comfort, the seats, the quiet cabin, not to say hey, look what I'm driving.

What sort of message does this send to your children who don't just get everything they need but everything they *want*? He always remembered growing up that his older brother Peter used to believe that you live for today, get everything you can, now, and don't worry about tomorrow or anyone else for that matter.

Steve had always been different, more serious, concerned about social justice, trying to solve the world's problems. His parents and relatives had seen that in him ever since he was a freshman in college when a girl who was his first love wanted to change the world and didn't, but she changed him.

Then meeting Becky, a social worker who always believed you have to help change society, not wait for someone else to do so. And not just write out a check or hit the "donate here" button online. Together they did that, volunteering for countless organizations, raising thousands of dollars over the course of a lifetime, helping out at their synagogue. God, why can't these values pass on to our kids and their kids? L'dor v'dor as they say in Hebrew.

He enters a grocery supermarket to pick up some cut-up watermelon and cantaloupe pieces and as he leaves, he sees four migrants huddled against the store wall with a crude sign reading Can You Help Us-From Venezuela? A father, mother and two girls sit with nothing but a couple of half empty water bottles and food wrappers in front of them. Steve walks over and hands the wife a five-dollar bill.

"Gracias, senor. You older people understand."

Steve shakes his head. "No senora. I understood when I was much younger." This was a sign to Steve. And not the kind on a piece of cardboard.

That Friday night Lori called him while he was taking a walk.

"Daddy, thank you so much!"

"For what, Lori? Did I send a check or something?"

"No silly, for Noel. Barry came over at about four and spent two hours with Noel. Pitching to him, adjusting his swing. Your grandson was the happiest I've seen since, since, well, you know."

"That makes my day Lori, honey, it truly does. I'm happy he's happy and I'm actually proud of Barry," Steve replies. "Let's see if it pays off at all tomorrow morning."

"Oh, I bet so. It can only help. And Barry was so good about it all. I asked if he wanted to stay for dinner, but he had plans at his golf club with some guys."

"Of course he did," Steve said. Does a bear shit in the woods? He thought.

"Well, I'll see you tomorrow, and thanks again. Oh, by the way, isn't tomorrow your big date? You'll like her, she's so nice, and pretty. I'm amazed someone hasn't snatched her up."

"I agree, but that kind of begs the question, I mean, what would she see in me? I'm not very nice or pretty."

"You'll be fine, dad, just be yourself, compliment her and be interested in what she has to say. And oh, let the past rest. Women don't want to be compared to a guy's divorced or dead wife."

"Jesus Lori, I haven't dated in many years, but I know that much."

"I know you do Dad, just saying. See you tomorrow."

"Have a good night hon. Yes, see you tomorrow."

CHAPTER EIGHT

The next morning is a cloudy and breezy Saturday in June. If there was an announcer at the little league game, he would have said it was a perfect day for baseball, in between an ad for gutter guards and a car insurance company. To announcers, it was always a perfect day for baseball. Steve was in his usual spot in the first row of the bleacher seats, and he was early. The Yankees are taking fielding practice with Noel in right field as usual. Gordy Graff is at the plate hitting perfectly placed balls that he tosses up and hits to the various fielders. "Okay, ready positions everyone," Gordy sings out. The players lean forward, almost squatting.

Steve is actually trying to take his mind off the game, thinking about tonight, the date with Candace. He should text her to confirm that it's on, but it's only nine-twenty and that would show he's overanxious and possibly rude. She could still be asleep. What should he wear? Maybe that red polo shirt with thin tan stripes and tan pants. And brown Skechers. Okay. Sounds good. He would wear a pair of moccasins he's had for a while, but they hurt his feet and his back. No support. You gotta have support.

The coach hits a grounder left of the second baseman who can't reach it in time. Noel fields it cleanly and throws it to second base to hold the imaginary runner at first. Lori slips in next to Steve. She looks better today, neatly dressed in a blue jumper with her hair done in a pageboy style and some makeup. Like he told Barry, if she's not miserable, then neither am I.

"Hi Daddy, did it start yet?"

"Nope, they're just finishing up some practice."

After hitting a perfectly placed fly ball to center, the coach does the same to Noel in right. He comes in a little bit and catches it, covering the ball in his glove with his free hand, just as he was taught.

"Daddy, you have to call Barry and thank him, no matter what happens today."

"Lori, I know. I'm in my seventies, not seven. I'll call him later." And if I'm lucky, I'll get his voicemail, he thought. Then he thought how horrible that was and decided if he got voicemail, he'd just say to call him back.

The other team, the Cardinals, bat first and the game goes scoreless after two innings, rare in a young level little league game. Noel would probably bat in the third inning. It turned out he was eighth in the lineup. There was actually an Indian boy on the team, Dov, who was a worse hitter than Noel.

Steve was daydreaming about what to order at Emilio's tonight when Noel steps to the plate. Lori grabs his hand. "Oh, I hope and pray he gets a hit," she says. Steve swallows hard.

The first pitch is inside and Noel ducks away, but not as if he were scared, just naturally getting out of the way of the ball. That seemed different. The second pitch is low, and Noel doesn't swing. That seemed different as well, since he had been swinging at some awful pitches lately in an attempt to get his first hit before the season ran out. If nothing else, Barry had seemingly taught him some fundamentals.

On the third pitch, which is right over the plate, he steps into and strokes the ball with what looks like a picture book swing to left center field. Everyone is yelling, in Lori's case screaming, for him to run. Everyone except Steve, whose mouth has a gaping hole but with nothing coming out. The outfielders misplay the ball as Noel rounds second base heading for third. His teammates and the Yankees' parents, in the stands, are cheering. His best friend Taren is waving his hat at him, and Gordy Graff shakes his head while applauding at the same time. "That's the way Noel, great hustle, you got it buddy," he yells.

Steve turns to Lori and finally speaks. "Unbelievable," was all he could say. Noel would score on a single two batters later as the coach greets him out of the dugout area near home plate and pats his cap when he takes off his helmet.

In his second at bat, two innings later, on the first pitch, he hits a hard-line drive to the short stop who drops the ball but picks it up and throws to first. Noel is out by two steps. His coach yells to him, "That's okay, Noel, way to hustle. Way to hustle."

It was the top of the sixth with the Yankees up three to two, and the Yankees at bat when the heavens open up and a cloudburst covers the field. But the game was official.

Everyone scatters. No time for congratulations, just get to the cars. Steve and Lori wait for Noel in place, rain be damned. Noel scrambles over into his mother's arms, dropping his glove at Steve's feet. Then he turns to Steve. "Papa, did you see my hit? I almost had two!" Then they hug, hard.

Steve's eyes are moist. "I'm so proud of you, bud, so proud." He then hugs Lori.

"Thank you, Dad," she whispers. "Thank you, thank you, thank you."

"It wasn't me, honey, I just put it in motion."

The ride home was wet, but Steve was happy and, more than happy, proud. Proud of his grandson and especially proud of his son. He pulls over to a gas station near downtown Westfield and fills up. Thank God I don't go anywhere, he thinks. This thing is a pig on gas. Before he pulls away, he texts Candace. HI, ARE WE STILL OK FOR 6:30? JUST MAKING SURE. He tries to carefully choose his words.

His phone immediately pings back. SURE THING! SEE U LATER! Followed by a thumb's up emoji.

He texts back. Great! Look for a large black SUV.

He heaves a sigh of relief through his soaked Illini T-shirt. He taps his phone in a holder and drives onto Dundee Road, heading west to the house. "Call Barry." The phone rings several times.

"Hello?"

"Hey Barry, it's Dad."

"Hey Dad. How are ya? I only got a few minutes. I'm in line at a car wash."

"Car wash? It just poured by me."

"I'm up in Lincolnshire. It poured here too, but now the sun's out."

Steve laughed, "You see opportunities, son."

Barry did the same. "Always Dad, always."

"Well, I just wanted to thank you. I'm coming from Noel's little league game this morning."

"Yeah, he do okay?"

"Better than okay. He got a triple, even though the outfielders miffed it. And then he hit a sharp liner, which the shortstop dropped but managed to pick up and throw him out by a step. But he stepped into the ball, wasn't afraid of it and his swing was like watching you at that age, like perfect. I don't know what you did, but your sister thinks you walk on water and honestly, so do I."

Barry laughs. "Gee, that's great to hear. I don't know, just taught him some fundamentals, I guess. Teaching him to be smart about how he plays, that's all."

"Well, whatever you did," Steve shivers momentarily, "I'm proud of you, son."

There was silence for a few seconds and Steve would swear until his dying day that Barry choked up just a bit. "Thanks Dad. I really appreciate that. More than you know. I gotta run. I'm next in line here."

"Love ya Barry."

"Back at ya Dad."

The ride home the rest of the way is quiet. *At Last,* by Etta James is softly humming through the speakers as Steve pulls into the garage. He takes his clothes off, practically peeling his wet T-shirt and socks off, throwing everything into a laundry bag in the closet. He sits in his shower stall on the tiled seat and just lets the water pour over him. He thinks about friends who were gone as he does more and more since Becky passed. Contemporaries of his. Ed Stratton at the bank, seventy-four, Dennis Carcelli, a close client who developed so many subdivisions in suburban Chicago with Steve's name on their streets, Kaufman Drives or Kaufman Lanes in every one, seventy-three as he remembered. Jerry Weintraub, whose law firm had represented the bank for forty-plus years, seventy-five. And of course, Greg Orlov, friend of forty years, who he had golfed with, seen every action movie with a body count, and introduced him to firearms, seventy-seven. He looks at his hands and long arms, bony now. And he asks the same question over and over. How long have I got? If my health breaks down, when is long too long?

He dries off and is going to make a sandwich for lunch, but he feels tired. Hell, he thought. What have I done today except go to a baseball game and get gas? But the bed beckoned, so he lays down in his undershorts and pulls the covers over. He has a dream that he and his boyhood and college friend, Jeff Hirsh, who was a pharmacist in Surprise, Arizona until he recently died from a stroke, were back in grammar school riding their bikes east to the lake. But Jeff said they should detour down Sheridan Road to the Edgewater Beach Hotel. Steve asked why.

"Cause the Pittsburgh Pirates are staying there. You know that Kaufman, the visiting teams in town, all stay there when they play at Wrigley," Jeff answered.

"My dad loves the Pirates!" Steve replied.

"Well then, let's go," said Jeff, riding ahead of him. But like in most dreams, it never finishes, and he found himself looking out the window of an apartment building somewhere spying an old man with a cane sitting on a bench. Of course, he asked if it was himself, but then his phone rings. "Hello?" he says weakly.

"Dad, it's Michelle. I'm so sorry. Were you sleeping?" said Barry's wife. He felt embarrassed spying the clock on his nightstand: three forty-seven in the afternoon.

"Yeah honey, a little cat nap. How are you? What's up?"

"Not much. I just wanted to tell you that you really moved your son with what you said to him about Noel. He told me, and Dad, he was almost in tears."

"Oh, well I didn't want that. I just wanted to tell him that what he did worked. He gave him confidence, and he has new skills and that most of all," Steve gulped, "that I was proud of him. I guess I haven't said that for a while and that's on me."

"No, it's not. You have to deserve things and this time he deserved it, and you responded. Look, speaking of which, I know it's been hard on you because we all don't see each other as much as we used to and that's on us. We're gonna try to change that."

Steve thought for a second. "No Michelle, it's not on you. I mean, it's true, but we all have our own lives and things going on. It's simply the fact that your lives and where you're at are a lot busier and more complicated than mine is. Believe me, I understand."

"No Dad, when the smoke clears, we're still family and we should be together more, no matter how busy or what the situation is."

He had always liked Michelle. She was a bit overweight, with dark skin and a beautiful face framed by dark hair. She had come from a traditional Jewish family, almost orthodox, but respected Barry's reform upbringing. She had a strong will and was conservative in beliefs, dress, and spending money. Steve often said thank God she reigns Barry in. "I appreciate it, Michelle. It's nice to hear."

"I mean it, you know I do. How's everything else?"

"Oh fine, I'm keeping busy." He didn't want to say he had a date tonight. That would be far too exhausting.

"Great, well, I've got to pick Randy up from a practice."

"Good to hear from you dear, give my love to the boys and thank you for calling. It means a lot to me."

"Of course, love you, Dad."

"Back at ya." To coin a phrase from his son.

CHAPTER NINE

Steve takes another shower as he awoke from his nap bathed in sweat. He puts on his red shirt with the thin tan stripes and tan pants, brushes back his gray hair and stares into the mirror asking the question he has asked a thousand times before, do I still look good enough to be attractive to someone of the opposite sex and of course he had no answer. He had put on a few pounds since his last physical and was shorter than his former six feet two lanky frame, probably closer to six feet.

He puts on a brown weave leather belt and slips into a pair of brown Skechers, loads up his pockets and checks the Post-It note that he taped to the frame of the door leading to the garage that he put up last year because he thought he was forgetting things when he left the house: glasses, wallet, phone, house keys, car keys, pen. More and more of his friends were doing this as they entered their seventies. Not as an indication of anything, maybe just a precaution.

Then he dashes back into the house and into a dresser drawer in his bedroom, fumbling through clothes and reaching into the back where he finds it: a bottle of cologne. Mont Blanc. He dusts it off and tries to remember who the hell gave it to him years back. He didn't remember it from the funeral or sitting Shiva for Becky. Whatever. He puts a spritz on his wrists and a bit on each side of his neck.

Okay, got everything and it's five-forty, let's roll. He puts the AC on low and drives out of the subdivision, looking twice in the vanity mirror to check how he had shaved. He wears glasses for distance and wonders if he should keep them on when meeting Candace. Didn't it hide any bags or circles under his eyes? Oh, stop it. Up the street to Lake Cook Road, east to Waukegan Road, making every light, shit, I'm going to be too damn early and what if there's no parking on Second Street, hell it's downtown Highland Park, I'll be circling the block for half an hour, slow down.

He goes east off Waukegan down Deerfield Road going very slow, it was known to be a speed trap anyway and when the road curves north he pulls into a shopping center parking lot, figuring he has about ten minutes to kill. With the engine idling he turns on the radio and what was playing? *Under Pressure* by David Bowie and Queen, unbelievable. He can't wait ten minutes, make it eight. He pulls out and follows the road across the Edens Expressway, where it turns into Central Avenue in Highland Park. Six-twenty now. Well, maybe she's downstairs early. He turns south down Second Street. The nav says one more block. It's almost six twenty-five.

And there she was. Coming out of her building with a wide wave, wearing a cute, printed blouse with a scarf across it and black dress pants. Shoulder-length blond hair and big brown eyes, reminding him of a special girl from college many years ago. Get out and get the door for her dumb ass. Put your four-ways on first. By the time the step came out and he ran around to the passenger side, she was by the door.

"Uh, hi!"

"Hi, you didn't have to do that. The street's bad here."

"Oh no problem," as he opens the door, the step comes out below the door.

"Fancy," she said. "But nice, I've a sore hip right now."

"Really? Me too. We seem to already have something in common." That sounded dumb and presumptuous.

She laughs as they both close their doors, and he pulls away to drive around the block back to Central. "You look great," he says.

"Well, thank you," she replies in that cheery voice. "So do you. I realized you have to double back here tonight, and you live in Westfield. I could have driven and met you there."

"Nah, it's fine," he waves a hand at her. It's not really that far from here and parking is tight over there, so one car is fine. "Have you been there recently?" This isn't too bad, he thinks.

"Oh, about, let's see," she closes her lips, and her eyes move from side to side, thinking, "Maybe four years ago, with some friends. It was good, but I heard they changed the layout. You?"

"Almost a year back. Yes, they did, made the dining room bigger. I don't remember what I had to eat, just that I didn't have a great time."

"Oh, how come?" She looks at him and cocks her head. She is so pretty and seems to be hanging on his every word.

"I was with another couple; they asked me to go with them. My wife had just passed. They thought they were being nice, and they were, but it was very awkward." Why did you bring this up? Does she want to hear this? Of course not.

"That's right, Linda told me. And when I'd see Lori, she would always go on about her, how she was 'a volunteer's volunteer' and didn't have an enemy in the world. Breast cancer, wasn't it?"

"Yeah, she had it back in 1981 when we were newlyweds, beat the odds and then forty-one years later it comes back." Get off of Becky! "And I understand your husband or ex-husband passed years back too?"

"Yep. Six months after we were divorced in 2021, a girlfriend of mine saw him on a date *while* we were married, if you can believe that. We were divorced and two months later he was diagnosed with liver cancer, stage four, and was gone two months after that. Yep, uh, huh."

"Wow. Can I ask, did he…"

"Drink? Oh yeah. Once in a while, then more than once in a while, then when the kids were at college and out of the house, more and more. Then he started coming home really late, and said he had to keep the store open late. He owned a jewelry store on Wabash downtown on Jewelers' Row, so I knew that was crap."

"So even if you had stayed married, it might have happened anyway?"

"Oh definitely."

Steve finds a space in back of the restaurant and she laughs and says, "You don't have to get the door. I'm fine and I see this step takes a while to come up, though it's really cool."

He laughs and says, "Okay."

They go in through the back of the restaurant and Steve flags down the hostess. They were just clearing a booth for them (he had requested this when making the reservation) and they scoot in. He keeps looking at her. She is very pretty and looks younger than seventy-two, except for some wrinkles and crow's feet around her eyes which age her a bit. But the whole situation, being on a date, being in this restaurant, seems dreamlike.

She scans the room as he scans her. "You know it's funny. Ever see what couples do when they sit down?" she asks.

"What's that?" he replies.

"See, some sit down next to each other and others across

from each other."

"Gosh, I never noticed. I guess I like to look at whom I'm talking to. Does that make sense?" He hoped he was saying the right thing. It sounded right, practical, but not exactly passionate.

"No, I agree. But some people feel the need to be next to each other. They think it makes them more connected."

Whew, he thought. But sound interested, give her options. "Would you want me to..."

"Oh no, you're fine," she smiles.

"Oh good. So, tell me about yourself, Mrs. Miller."

And she did.

He orders chianti, and she has spring water with a lemon. They order egg-plant parmesan and lasagna and tried each other's dishes and ended up splitting them like an old married couple. Then they split a piece of tiramisu for dessert. He asks about her perfume, and she said it was Versace, Bright Crystal, and he said he liked the smell. She thought he smelled nice and asked what he had on, and he told her how he found the bottle of Mont Blanc in his dresser and dusted it off with no idea how he got it. He told her he had a couple of Mont Blanc pens but never knew they made cologne, and she laughed at that, a kind of titter.

They talk about everything past the plate clearing and the check being put on the table in the folder. About families, about life, and they seemed to agree on many, many things.

The one hiccup occurred when she brought up her older and only brother, Carl. Her eyes narrow and he sees a side of her that seems to seethe with a deep resentment for him as her parents thought he could do no wrong and growing up, it was always about what Carl was doing or did, never about her. Her dad traveled a lot on business and when he'd call home it was always what's Carl up to? Did he throw touchdowns as the quarterback? Meanwhile, she went to the finals downstate twice on her school's tennis team, but her parents seldom showed up to a game.

Steven remembers what Lori said: listen, empathize, commiserate. And he did, saying how awful that was and that he sort of went through the same thing with his older brother Peter until his parents realized what a screw up he was. She laughed at that, and he said how tragedy is often the source of laughter.

He knows it sounds like bullshit, but as they got back to the car, he actually says to her that what he was about to say will sound phony, but how was she still 'available' given her looks and personality? She titters and says he was a newbie and that dating and finding someone wasn't as easy for her as he might think. He asks if she would forgive him for the remark. It was his ignorance after so many years of never having to date.

She says she completely understands and says, of course. As they pull up to her building, there was a loading zone he parks in.

"Parking's really bad here. It's like the city."

"I know. I have this issue with friends all the time," she answers.

He slaps his knee and turns to look at her. "Well, Candace, I've got two questions for you. The second kind of depends on the first." He's smiling, but also apprehensive.

"Ok Steven, fire away." She's smiling too.

"Did you have a good time?"

"I did. Great place and great company. You did fine."

"Okay, then number two, would you like to go out again?"

"I would."

"That's great, uh, thanks."

A siren blares for a second and startles them both. A Highland Park Police Department Unit pulls up next to him. The cop on the passenger side rolls down his window, as does Steve. The officer says nothing but gives him a look like you know it's a loading zone and you know you gotta move, and Steve just nods back.

"Oh brother," Candace says. "Will you call me, and we can talk?"

"Sure, when's good?"

"Well, I'm a little tired. It's what, nine-fifteen? How about in an hour or so?"

He laughs; a bit startled. "Oh, sure, you got it." He reaches over and puts his arm around her, and they kiss and he inhales the Versace Bright Crystal. She smiles and makes that little titter laugh as she opens the door and the step comes down.

"Bye," she smiles.

"Bye," he smiles. That titter is annoying, but he thinks he could get used to it.

He thinks that went well, but doesn't want to get ahead of himself. Maybe she was nice but didn't really like him and had trouble telling guys that. But that he should call in an hour? That's got to be good, right? He didn't want to be too happy, so when *Knee Deep* came on the radio by the Zac Brown Band (featuring Jimmy Buffett) and he would normally sing along he switches to the classical station and tried to relax to Vivaldi's violins of *The Four Seasons.* Then he pulls into the garage, he looks at the car clock and it's close to ten. Not an hour yet, so he goes in and takes his shirt off and waits for the news to come on. Right after the sports part of the news, he calls.

She has the same news channel on in the background when he calls, and they start to talk about TV and movies and everything else. They get off at close to midnight, both starting to yawn. He says he'll call her tomorrow. As he hangs up the phone, he realizes that they never discussed where to go or what they wanted to do next.

CHAPTER TEN

The next day Steve plays golf in the morning at Ivanhoe and plays well, but his mind was still on last night. He goes home and makes up a shopping list, then takes a nap for half an hour before driving to Mariano's off of Willow Road. It has been a while now that he has shopped for one person, and it was sometimes hard. He used to go to Sunset Foods with Becky, but he couldn't walk in the store since she died. Now he'd see items on sale if you bought like three or five of something and although friends would tell him to buy things and freeze them to stock up, it just seemed like too much effort.

After skipping the last few aisles, he finds a short checkout lane, empties his cart in his cargo space in the back of the SUV and speeds home. By the time he puts everything away, his back starts up and he slips into an easy chair ready to watch Sixty Minutes and have a late dinner, his phone rings. Oh no, Lori.

"Hi Daddy, how are you?"

"Just sitting down. It's been a long day."

"On the golf course, come on Dad."

"I shopped after that and I'm tired, really tired."

"Well, I'll just be a sec. It's about next Sunday. It's Noel's birthday, and he's having a friend-party on Saturday, but I wanted to get the family together on Sunday. I'm asking Barry and Michelle as well. I'm bringing in from either Judy's or Lou Mal's, haven't decided yet."

"Sure, can I pitch in on the food?"

"No, Dad, you always ask me that. I'm doing fine. Work is good and Shelly's finally caught up with support payments. Oh, and the other thing. What did you *do* last night?" she asks in an almost accusatory tone.

"Whaddya mean?" he almost stutters, wondering what she means about the date. See, he thinks, I knew it was too good to be true. I screwed it up; I just knew it.

"You apparently made a wonderful impression on your date, from what Linda told me. She really, really liked you and had a great time."

"Oh, yeah, I did too. I was out of practice, but I did like you said, listened, sounded and actually *was* interested in what she was saying and only mentioned mom when she asked about her," he said this with a huge sigh of relief.

"Well, Mr. Kaufman, she sounded pretty taken by whatever you said or did. Did you ask her out again?"

"Umm, not exactly. You see, she wanted me to call her after the date when I got home so we could talk about what to do and where to go next."

"That's great! A wonderful sign! And did you do that?"

"Yeeeah, I called her but we kind of got sidetracked talking about a lot of different things and by the time we hung up, I realized we didn't make plans."

"Well, why are you just sitting there? You're home now. Call her! I can't believe you waited this long! She'll get a totally wrong signal from you!"

"Lori, I will, I will. I'm not a child. I'll call her. Believe me, I will."

"And I'm hanging up now, so you can do just that. Noel's next game is Wednesday at Village Green, four-thirty. Call her!" She hangs up.

He waits until after dinner and calls her but gets her voice mail. He apologizes for not calling sooner and asks if she would like to go to the Studio Five in Evanston, where they have jazz groups playing, because she told him she liked jazz. He mentions this and asks if she could call back. He then realizes the jazz groups there were on Fridays, not Saturdays. Old minds.

She calls back in twenty minutes and suggests a different idea. How would he like one of those home-cooked meals he misses so badly? Of course, he says yes, and she asks him what he would like. He says, how about seafood, nothing fancy? And she says great. She wants him to come early, around five o'clock, because of the traffic madness in her neighborhood. He indicates that wouldn't be a problem. He asks what he could bring, and she suggests wine. A white, he thought. He had bottles upon bottles of wine from a wine club Barry had him join. Sweet or dry? Why not both or just ask her? So, he calls her back, but she said either one, so he said he'd bring both and she laughed, that titter. It was cute, but still annoying.

When you're alone and retired, your calendar frees up and you look forward to things, you formerly thought of as routine. Like the Wednesday night get-togethers at Stu's or a baseball game or Sunday golf. You look forward to them because *you're with people,* you thrive around them. People with partners or your kids don't get that. The Wednesday night boys do.

When Becky was dying, Steve wished and hoped that every day was twice as long, that they could have more time together, even towards the end when he would just sit by her and watch her lifeless body and labored breathing. God, even if it was miserable to watch and to be there, he would pray for another week, another day, another hour.

And now the times to see people couldn't come fast enough. So, Monday when Stu called about Wednesday, Steve was actually excited. After all, there was the murder to discuss and, of course, where were they going to order from. Little things.

"I was thinking of Chinese, specifically Hong Minh in Glenview," Stu said.

"I'm in. I love their egg rolls, big and crisp," Steve replied.

"Okay, so you want that and your beef and broccoli?"

"You got it. Want to split an order of fried rice?"

"Okay," Stu said, "but I like the pork fried rice, despite what my rabbi would say."

Steve snickers. "Yeah, yeah. You've used that one before. Okay."

"Also got an announcement to make for you guys," Stu sounds serious.

"What, is it personal or something? You moving to Arizona to be near your sister?"

"No, but it is personal."

"You're not going to tell each of us by phone, but make a dramatic thing about it at your house?"

"That's exactly what I'm going to do," he said, again sounding very serious.

"Okay, see you then," replies Steve, really curious now.

"It will be worth the wait," Stu answers.

"I bet." And now Wednesday really couldn't come soon

enough.

CHAPTER ELEVEN

Wednesday morning saw Steve grumbling from a backache. Driving to Gat Guns all the way in East Dundee was out of the question, heated and massaging car seats or not. Hell, driving just to Maxom's in Des Plaines was too far. He has a light breakfast and, for some reason, pops three Cyclobenzaprine tablets and goes back to bed.

When he wakes up, it is three forty-seven on his nightstand clock. "Shit!" Noel's game is at four! His back feels better, so he brushes his teeth, throws on a Northwestern tee and cargo shorts and leaves the house. The sky to his west looks not just cloudy but very dark, and he thinks he hears the rumbling of thunder.

About halfway to the ballfield, heavy drops start splattering his windshield. He finds a parking space about a block away and trots to the field. He couldn't run anymore since the back surgery; thank heaven he could still play golf, but his long legs help get him there quickly. But just as he arrives, the home plate umpire calls the game. Home plate umpire, a job he had in high school and his son did too.

"Daddy, where were you?" Lori asked as she covered him with her umbrella while he spots Noel and some other players packing up the team's equipment.

"Uh, my back was killing me this morning, so I took a

muscle relaxer and fell asleep. Just literally woke up twenty minutes ago."

"Well, the game just went two innings, no score, but your grandson hit a single."

"That's great Lori. I'm happy to hear it."

"So, I'm going to wait for Noel. Why don't you wait and we can all share an umbrella. Where'd you park?"

"I'm way down the street. It's okay, I'll wait to say hello and then scram. I have to shower anyway."

"Oh, that's right, the Wednesday night boys, right?"

"Yep, Chinese tonight from Hong Minh's."

Lori looked at him slyly. "Oh, great egg rolls. Got a second date Saturday at Candace's house, huh? Home cooking, I understand?" A huge smile crosses her face.

"Jesus, Lori, does all of Westfield know?" he said half smiling, half irritated.

"And probably Highland Park," she giggled.

Noel saves the day. "Hi Papa, no score, but I got a hit. Clean single. We'll have to make the game up sometime next week."

"I heard. That's great. Not too many left, huh?"

"I think three or four. Then the playoffs start, double elimination."

The rain was coming down harder if that was possible.

"All right guys, love ya." Steve sprints to the car. Luckily his tee was drip dry.

"Bye Dad, have fun Saturday!" Lori called.

"Bye Papa, see you soon," Noel yelled.

Steve waves and continues trotting when he spots the water beads on his car. Good wax job he thinks. And now of course it rains.

Stu had texted everyone to come at about six forty since he was in Glenview picking up the food for tonight and would be a bit late. Fine with Steve, a few extra minutes to practice his golf swing against the net he had set up in his basement with his new Calloway sand wedge, a Father's Day gift from the kids last year.

Stu has all the food containers on the kitchen table when Steve walks in. Al Diamond is already there rummaging through what he ordered, and they can all hear Mike Baricello's car entering the driveway.

People were eating quickly. Some were just hungry, but all wanted to know what Stu's big announcement concerned. When the egg rolls, beef with broccoli, Mongolian beef, egg foo young, three kinds of fried rice, moo shu pork, and finally the almond and fortune cookies had all been devoured and the table cleared, everyone adjourns to the living room.

Stu excuses himself and comes back with three eight by ten photographs of himself with an Asian woman and passes them out. "Fellas, this is Ann Chen. She's my girlfriend. We've been seeing each other for a couple months now. I introduced her to my family Sunday night here at the house. She's forty-six and a dentist in Park Ridge. We love each other and I figured it's time we came out in the open, as it was."

"Holy shit Stu," said Mike. "What took you so long?

"Congratulations!" Al said.

"Wow," was all Steve could manage, thinking she was quite beautiful but also that she was a year older than Barry.

Stu goes through the story of how they met at Starbucks, all the dates they'd been on and yes, they had been intimate. It took a while for it to sink in on three elderly guys but at least openly they were extremely happy for Stu and perhaps a bit envious of him.

Stu said it went well with the family although he could see the doubt on his kids' faces. Then he told them how they loved each other, were happy and that they all had to live with it. The other three agreed completely nodding and more 'good for you' remarks.

Mike, the detective of the group, asks why she had never been married, and Stu gave everyone a background history of how she *was* married once before in an arranged marriage which lasted less than a year where the groom was seldom home with a bad gambling addiction and missing work and a home life. Steve could certainly relate to that from his former son-in-law and said so. After a bit of further conversation on Ann Chen they moved to the status of the Heller murder, all eyes on Mike.

"They interviewed Sheila and Nathan, searched the condo and took their phones and laptops. Nothing critical there. They were together the night of the murder watching TV but that's kind of convenient. They were very defensive at being persons of interest."

"Well naturally," said Al. "They're damned if they seem unaffected and on the other hand grief and over-concern could be looked at as just an act."

"Yeah, Sheila got a bit nasty, especially when one of the detectives asked her point blank 'Didn't you kind of wish for this?' to which she picked up a Lalique statue and almost hurled it at him before thinking about it and putting it back down," Mike responds.

"She probably realized at the last split second that insurance wouldn't pay for it if she did that," Stu offered. Mild laughter all around.

Mike went on. "They've got all Jack's files. Heller and Morris. Jack and Steve Morris represented mob Outfit guys going back years. Most recently Jack represented Albert Caruso and Chris Spino, part of the mob's Grand Avenue Crew. Both were found guilty of racketeering and second-degree murder, and both were appealing their sentences. Jack and another firm were representing them on appeal."

"Well, they wouldn't want to whack their lawyer during an appeal, would they? That makes no sense," says Al.

"Right," answers Mike. "But hold on. Jack also represented a couple of Outfit guys in the Chinatown crew, David and Mike Caruso, brothers, no relation to Albert. Last year David got fifteen to twenty on a RICO charge, but Mike got off, same case, same facts. And Dave's nephew Danny, Mike's son, is supposedly really pissed at Jack about it. The FBI and Chicago P.D. are hauling his ass in for questioning. So, there's that lead."

"Wait a minute Mike," Stu pipes in. "Hold on a second. Are you telling me these Outfit guys still go around whacking people because of some grievance or they're afraid someone's going to flip on them or something? I thought that crap was over with years ago."

"You'd be surprised at the shit that still goes on, Stu." Mike crosses his arms and shakes his head. "People think that because these guys aren't in the headlines anymore that stuff doesn't happen. Well, it's not like it used to be but it still does on occasion." The room was quiet for a minute with everyone nodding.

"There's something else though, I've saved the best for last," Mike continues. "Although they know the cars were different at the scene, they did find something when they searched Nathan's Camaro and Sheila's Lexus." Mike pauses for effect as everyone leans in. "Behind some clothing in Nate's trunk was a Glock 19, same type of gun used to shoot Jack. They're running ballistics tests on it now."

This was followed by a 'No shit,' 'Really?' and 'Oh my gosh,' in that order.

"But that's not all. Sheila's car had a scrap of paper in the glove box with the name 'Johnny' on it followed by a 773-area code phone number. A number trace links it to Johnny Rossi, an Outfit guy who works with the Grand Avenue Crew. They tried to find him and apparently the guy just disappeared without a trace."

"What?" Steve almost yells.

"This gets better and better," replies Al.

"So they think she might have hired this guy for a hit on Jack?" Stu asks.

"Hey, it certainly looks like a possibility," Mike says.

"But say it's true," Steve points at Mike, "Why the hell would she keep that note and in a glove compartment no less? And if Nate is the shooter, why wouldn't he have disposed of the gun? It makes no sense."

"Don't know. They're dusting the cars for prints, not that they'll find anything. When asked about the gun and the note they both went ballistic, denied any involvement saying they were being framed and were contacting their lawyer who just happens to be Steve Morris. Her car is parked in the condo garage, his is in the outside parking lot. Lots of questions right now, few answers."

They talk about the case and a few other things but by nine thirty everyone is starting to leave. All again congratulated Stu. You either thought it was great, he was nuts, or you were envious. Steve thought all three.

As he enters the house and grabs some stale leftover popcorn from a bowl, his phone rang. A 702-area code. Normally he'd let it go, but he realizes his brother Peter lives in Vegas and that's their area code although the number doesn't look familiar.

"Hello?"

"Hi, is this Steve, Steve Kaufman?"

"It is."

"Hi Steve, my name's Amy, Amy Klein. I'm your brother Peter's girlfriend."

"Okay, hi Amy, what's up? You sound rattled." He didn't know about Amy, but this figured with Peter.

"I am kind of. Your brother, he, he had a heart attack yesterday, he's in University Hospital here in Vegas. He had always said to me if anything happened to him that I should call you. So, I am."

"Oh my gosh, is he okay?"

"Yes, they put a shunt in his valve and he's pretty stable, but I'm pretty sure he'd want you to know."

"Yes, thanks. I appreciate that. Let me see if I can get a flight out there tomorrow."

"Oh, okay, well that would be nice. He's stable, alert, but that would be great if you could come."

"I'll book a flight when we hang up." Steve then asks her to confirm her phone number. He finds a nine fifty-five flight to Harry Reid Airport and a return flight to O'Hare at ten-fifteen. Then he calls Tony, an Uber driver he knew and had used and confirms the pickup time for the morning. Truth be told he never cared for Las Vegas, thought it was a vacation spot for the hoi polloi and he could never hang around with his seventy-seven-year-old brother for very long in any case.

CHAPTER TWELVE

It's raining Thursday morning when Tony arrives in his immaculate black Toyota Camry. He'd last seen Tony about a month ago when he picked him up for a golf trip to Hilton Head. Tony was an interesting guy. A Lebanese immigrant who lived in Dallas for five years, he came up to Chicago to live with his daughter in Glen Ellyn after his wife died. She had an executive position at Rush Hospital, and he figured he could drive a cab or an Uber or a Lyft anywhere and he was right. A very righteous man, not so much religious, which was good for Steve, putting him at ease with Tony's Muslim faith, but someone who believed and preached hard work without any shortcuts to success. Tony also believed in social justice, a deep-seated belief of Steve Kaufman, which he had held going back even before his marriage to Becky Dean.

"Mr. Steve, do you want me to call my cousin to take you from the Vegas airport to the hospital?" Steve had found that Tony had a relative in almost every major city in the U.S. who was somehow involved in the 'transportation' business.

"Yeah, sure Tony, if he can do it, that would be great."

"Of course he can. I'll give you his number before I let you off at American Airlines."

They rode on to the airport with Tony complaining about

college kids not learning anything useful and getting into trouble with the law. Steve is tired and, for the most part, just agrees with him. When they pull up to an American departure gate, Tony hands him, his business card with his cousin's name and number scribbled at the bottom. "I wish I could pick you up tonight, but I've got my nephew's high school graduation," Tony says as Steve exits the car.

"Not a big deal," Steve replies. "I'll catch an Uber or a cab." He finds an airline employee walking around and she helps him get his boarding pass. If you're a senior, many times if you just stand and look around with a befuddled look on your face, people assume you need help. Usually, they're right. He asks her if it was very far to the gate as he couldn't walk far due to back issues. She assures him it isn't.

The flight is uneventful, and he mostly reads a Steven King novel on his Kindle or tries to sleep, which he actually does. When they land, he goes to the nearest arrival terminal and calls Tony's cousin Semi and then Amy.

"I won't be there until two," Amy says. "I work part time at the sheriff's office."

"Okay, well, I'll see you then. I'm heading over right from the airport."

"Sure, that'll be great."

Peter had been married years ago, then divorced, never had any kids. Frankly, Steve had become tired of hearing about all his girlfriends through the years. This was even true back in college. But he's your brother and now he needs your support. Or so you think.

Semi is a young guy, clean cut with a mustache. Steve has to laugh; he seems like a younger version of Tony. He is going to UNLV part time to learn programming. The ride takes about twenty minutes when Semi pulls up to the large glass curved entrance to UNLV Hospital and Medical Center. Semi couldn't get Steve tonight either. He had class, but he gives Steve a slip of paper with a name and number on it, Ali, another cousin.

Steve finds his way to an information desk and asks for the room number for Peter Kaufman. He signs in, is given a visitor badge, and finds the elevator to the fifth floor. Signs direct him to five twelve and there in a private room is Peter, thinner than he imagined, with not much gray hair left, watching *The Price is Right* on a wall mounted TV.

"Hey little brother!" Peter almost yells, grabbing the remote to turn off the TV.

Steve grabs his outstretched arm.

"What the hell are you doing here?" he asks. They both grin, Peter more broadly.

Steve grabs a chair next to a nightstand and pulls it up near the bed.

"Oh, had a bit of a ticker issue. Was at the office closing a deal on a 2020 Range Rover, on the phone with a guy, and all of a sudden it got all dark and I had this massive pain in my chest and in my jaw. Luckily, someone on the showroom floor saw through the glass into my office and watched me collapse. He managed to get me to sit up and called nine-one-one. So here I am. A couple of valves were clogged up, and I had a double bypass due to some clogged arteries, no big deal."

"My God, so if your office wasn't glass, that might have been it."

"Yep. Or if this guy who works for us wasn't right there in front of the office. But I guess it would have happened sometime, huh? I mean, it took Dad, now me, so you're next." Peter chortles at his own joke.

"Gee thanks, you putz." They both laugh. "So, tell me what

else is new. How's life been treating you and who's Amy? She said you just had a shunt."

"That's what I told her at first. Didn't want to scare her. Life's okay. This dealership I'm in with two other guys is great. Used high end cars are big here. Should have done it years ago. I mean, we used to sell brand new Cadillacs, GMCs, and Hummers, but the mark up on used cars is so much more."

"Your partners good guys?" Steve asks.

"Yep. One goes back to college with me at Dartmouth, the other's an Italian guy from out here."

Steve raises an eyebrow but says nothing.

"Now, why do people always think that?" Peter says, frustrated at Steve's look.

"Well, is he?" Steve asks, half smiling.

"No, he's not." But then with a wry smile he adds, "maybe some people he knows, maybe not."

"Associates," Steve smiles now.

"Yeah, associates," Peter laughs.

"And Amy?" Steve asks. "Don't give me your bull shit that she's the one."

"I would never say that. Wonderful girl, though. Okay, she's in her late fifties, divorced with a couple of kids. I met her at the dealership. She came in looking for wheels and we hit it off. Got her own place in Henderson. Her twin boys are down at ASU. She looks after me."

Steve puts his hands out in defense. "Hey, whatever makes you happy."

"Well, she does. And what about you? What's new back home?"

"Everything's okay. Lori's getting by okay. Her kids are growing."

"Is that prick paying her?" Peter snarls. "I know you're chipping in."

"Now he is. She's teaching and finally doing okay."

"I wanted to kill that mother, Steve. Leaving her like that. And I would have if you hadn't told me no. And I know cause I heard you wanted to do the same, even though you're mister righteous banker, pillar of the community. It was eating at you."

"Yeah, it was," was all Steve could muster to say. "You hate to see your child and grandchildren go through something like that."

"I never liked him, never trusted him. Mom and Dad always thought she could do better. Anyway, how's Barry? He's the man, isn't he?"

"He's fine. Busy life. I try to keep him from becoming too self-absorbed, like you."

"Oh, cut it out. So, give me some gossip from back on the North Shore."

"Well, the biggest news if you haven't heard is Jack Heller's murder."

Peter nods. "I've been following that. Closely. At first, they thought it was Sheila and their kid. What's his name?"

"Nathan."

"Yes, Nathan. But now they've turned their attention to some Outfit guys and think the wife and son might be framed. Am I right?"

"You know a lot, big brother. They found a note in Sheila's glove compartment that had a mob guy's name and phone number on it, but he's disappeared and then possibly they uncovered the murder weapon in Nathan's trunk."

"I heard that. Don't ask me how. And it was an Outfit guy. But you probably get your info before anyone because you see Mike Baricello, who I bet is working the case. What was the name on the note, Jimmy Rosa or Rossi?" Peter snaps his fingers, trying to think.

"Johnny Rossi. And he disappeared. No one can find him. But they do know that a yellow 2023 Dodge Charger was the car used by the murderer and Nathan's got a 2023 Camaro, which also happens to be yellow." Steve starts to think he's saying too much, but then Peter drops a bomb.

"That's funny. We just sold a yellow 2023 Charger that went to Chicago. I think the name was Rossi." Peter is struggling to remember the details. "I think it had a Wentworth Avenue address, but I'm not sure. I didn't personally handle the sale but..."

The phone rings. Peter grabs it. "Hello? Oh yeah, hi honey, I'm just here with my little brother catching up. Where are you? Oh, nuts, okay, well as soon as you can then. Bye."

Steve looks at him quizzically.

"That was Amy. She got held up at a meeting in the office."

Steve winces in his chair and grabs his back in
pain.

"Still bothers you, huh?" Peter asks.

"Yeah, two fusions and there are still days, like now, when it's tough."

Peter continues. "Well, I remember the sale. Thirty-five thousand paid plus ten and a quarter sales tax because the buyer lived in Illinois. You know I liked Jack Heller. He helped me out of a domestic matter after my divorce. A woman I went out with accused me of assault. Jack got me out of it."

"I'd love to help find who killed him. Just don't know what else I can do except listen to what Mike has to report," says Steve.

"I agree," replies Peter. "You know the buyer had to pay by check or wire cause he's out of state. I can check what the source of what that was when I get out of here. Maybe it'll lead to something."

"How will that go down with your partner?"

"Like I said, I liked Jack. This shouldn't have happened. Those are in our corporate records. We all have access to them."

"Well, that would be something. Just let me know, day or night."

Two nurses appear, one or both are Filipino, one heavy set, one thin, the thin one leading the way.

"Mr. Kaufman, you have tests downstairs in a few minutes, and you are supposed to be resting!" the thin nurse scolds.

"I was resting until my brother from Chicago barged in. Angie, Imelda, meet Steve, my little brother."

"He don't look so little to me," the thin nurse says, chuckling. "Nice to meet you, but he has to go have tests and then needs to rest."

"That's fine by me. I really should be taking off," Steve replies as he gets up in considerable back pain.

"Aww, you're chasing him out." Peter crosses his arms in disgust. "When's your plane going back, anyway?"

"It's at four but that's okay," Steve lies. "I'll just grab something at the airport and make some calls." He hugs his brother, who hugs him back.

"Will you keep in touch?" Peter asks seriously.

"Of course. And you be in touch first, if you find anything out or not."

"I will. Too bad you didn't get to meet Amy."

Not what Steve's thinking, but he plays along. "I will."

"You know, life's short. We shouldn't be strangers."

Steve takes this in. "Peter, I can honestly say that's one of the smartest things you've probably ever said."

Peter starts to laugh and with that, Steve's out the door. He calls the airline and manages to get an aisle seat on a six thirty-five flight coming back. He then calls Ali to see if he can get him now or in enough time to make the flight. Ali replies that he can get him in half an hour. He's nearby but is getting a haircut.

Ali looks exactly like Sevi but without a mustache. He is very quiet except when his phone rings and he speaks in rapid Arabic. Steve arranges for his new flight, goes through security and finds a Burger King. He orders his favorite, honey mustard chicken wraps and a Sprite. He settles into a booth and calls Mike Baricello.

"Hey Mike, sorry to call around dinner, but I'm at the airport in Vegas on the way back from seeing my brother."

"No big deal, Steve. I'm gonna make something in a few. Not that hungry. What's up in Vegas?"

"Aww, my brother had a heart attack followed by a double bypass, so I paid him a visit."

"That's too bad, he okay?"

"Yeah, he'll be fine, but I had to call you because he told me something and I didn't want to forget it. It's about Jack Heller's murder, believe it or not."

"Okay, spill it, I'm listening."

"Well, he's been following the case see, and he tells me right before the nurses come in to take him for some tests that, wait, let me back up a step. He and his two partners sell high end used cars. He tells me one of his partners just sold a yellow 2023 Dodge Charger to someone in Chicago named Rossi. He couldn't remember the first name but remembers it went to a Chicago address on Wentworth Avenue. Any of that make sense?"

"It sure does. The Carusos are Outfit boys, remember? And most of them, except for Albert, run out of Chinatown. And where's Wentworth Avenue?" Mike asks.

"Sure, Chinatown," Steve answers.

"Well, a couple things happened Stevie boy," Mike continues. "The ballistics report on the Glock in Nathan's trunk came back, and it matches the bullets that killed Heller. So, Nathan *and Sheila* have been charged. Just happened this morning. They're fighting over their bond amount with the State's Attorney. Then a warrant issued on David Caruso to search his residence and his cell phones, but remember, he's in prison and his nephew Jim lives at the house and it's been three months since David went away so who knows if they'll find anything."

"I still don't believe Nathan and Sheila did this, Mike. I told you all I think they're being framed."

"They're looking at all angles, Steve, all angles. If the Outfit is involved, it could take years to figure things out, years. But I'm sure going to pass on your information on the car."

They hung up and Steve felt like falling asleep. He hadn't told Mike everything yet, but would wait on Peter. He buys a newspaper and reads it at the restaurant, then walks down to his gate. It was far, and he stops several times. He has a beer on the plane, reads Stephen King and tries to sleep but can't. After landing and finding an Uber, Lori calls him in the car. Their conversation is brief. She asks about her uncle and says to Steve that he sounds tired. He admits that he is more than usual.

The Uber driver is a young Mexican kid, seems nice but almost misses the Willow Road exit from the tollway. It was eleven-forty by the time Steve was home. He takes off his clothes, chugs some orange juice from the carton, pops a few pills for both pain and sleep along with it and realizes he hasn't brought in the mail. It can wait. A few bills and donation requests were all it could be.

His back feels better but his left arm is aching, which was unusual. After all, he hadn't carried any luggage and didn't remember any awkward movements. Well, he'd see if it was still bothering him in the middle of the night during one of several trips to the bathroom that you made if you were over seventy.

CHAPTER THIRTEEN

Noel and his best friend Taren are in Noel's family room playing Street Fighter ALPHA 2, Nintendo's newest game. Don't ask how eight-year-olds hooked it up to the big screen TV that dominates a large portion of the room. His sister Stephanie helped a bit, but she's only ten. She's more of an Xbox person, however, which is also hooked up to the TV.

The boys are on the floor with their legs crossed, not far from the TV. Taren keeps pushing his bangs out of his face, a feat while operating his controller. His parents said he can let his hair grow out longer while Noel's mom just made him get a rather short haircut.

"Do you miss your dad?" Taren suddenly asks.

"I did, but now not so much."

"What about like at the games and school stuff?" Taren says.

"Naa, he never went to my games, anyway. Said he was always away on business or working late," Noel says. "You hungry?"

"A little bit. Let's wait till this game ends. Did it bother you?"

"Sure, but there are other kids whose dads or moms don't show up to the games. They just drop them there and drive off. Look at Steve Gordon. I don't even think I know what his parents look like. But something about the situation does bug me now."

"What's that?" asks Taren.

"Well, see now my mom tells me that he wasn't out of town or on business during my games. He was out drinking and gambling. That bothers me."

"Like gambling for money?"

"Yeah, I guess. But now my Papa comes to the games. Coach Graff knows him and my Uncle Barry. Coach Graff says Papa is one of the most well-liked people in town."

"I've seen him at the games. He's tall but moves kind of slow."

"He had a couple of back surgeries. He used to play baseball, basketball, and was a runner in high school. Now he just golfs," Noel replies.

"Yeah, guys like your grandpa and mine are really old. He's your mom's dad, right?"

"Yep."

"Where's your dad's dad?" says Taren as he ends the game.

"He lives in Seattle. He's kind of sick. Cancer, I think. Don't see him too often." Noel is starting to become uncomfortable and wants to change the subject. "So, the playoffs start tomorrow. My Uncle Barry might stop by."

"He's the guy who gave you the hitting lesson, right? That'd be cool."

"Yep, he's never been to a game of mine. His sons, my cousins, are on the high school and junior high baseball teams and my uncle played college ball somewhere. I asked Coach Graff about my uncle cause he knows him too."

"What did he say?"

Noel shrugs his shoulders. "He says he's a player, whatever that means."

"What *does* that mean?" asks Taren. "Like a baseball player?"

"I dunno," Noel replies.

Just then, Stephanie comes in. "You guys gotta put everything away, Noel. Mom is coming by to take you to the dentist. Taren, she's dropping you off at home. Who won the game?"

"Taren always wins," says Noel. "I wish I was good at something."

"I don't know Noel. You've been ripping the cover off the ball lately," Taren answers.

"We'll see if it carries over to tomorrow," Noel says and nods.

CHAPTER FOURTEEN

Steve wakes up Friday morning with a blinding headache and his arm, which stopped hurting in the middle of the night, hurts again. Lori calls him around ten. "Hi Daddy, how are you feeling? You sounded awful last night. Are you going grocery shopping today since you were in Vegas yesterday?"

"I don't know yet, Lori. I've got a blinding headache and my arm hurts."

"Which arm, that could mean something?" she says.

"My left. It travels up my shoulder."

"Aren't you seeing the doctor in a couple of weeks?"

"Yes, for a physical and tests before that, blood and everything."

"Why don't you call and see if you can see him earlier?"

"Lori, honey, you have to book a physical like six months in advance."

"Well, tell them there's something wrong with you and you want to try to book an earlier appointment."

"I'm sure they're very concerned that something's wrong with me. When's Noel's game?"

"Four o'clock. Barry's coming too. Please call the doctor and let me know how you are later."

"Okay, okay. But it's a waste of time."

Steve has his doctor's office on speed dial, along with his ortho doctor and urologist. His regular doctor is the partner of his two prior doctors who retired within two years of each other. The practice was bought out by The North Suburban Health Care Group. They promised the doctors when they bought the practice that they would be working less, doing less paperwork, cutting down on rounds and out of office calls and be paid handsomely. As the partners who retired told him, they lied. Rounds did get cut, but the paperwork increased beyond belief. Their hours were actually longer, and doctors who weren't retiring pushed up their retirement dates or simply left the practice and went elsewhere. So did lots of staff, nurses and P.A's, who'd been there for years.

The last time Steve called his doctor to leave a question and have the doctor call him back, it took four days, from Monday morning to Thursday evening at seven-fifteen when the doctor called him from his car on his way home. That was about a month ago. One of the retired doctors he knew well, finally answered the same question for him Tuesday afternoon.

He used to be able to ask his doctor, and the doctor would reply in their new, updated health portal online. However, now you can't do that, it's not an option. All you can do through the portal is see present and past appointments, check test results and if you have a question for your doctor, the only thing you can do in the portal is make a new appointment and who knows when someone will reply. How convenient. The state of 21st century medicine in America.

Hence the dreaded phone call. After listening to a long recording, he chooses to reach the message center. Someone answers and before he can even state that he's an existing patient who wants to see if he can schedule an earlier appointment, the person in messaging has asked at least five questions. She finally says the message will be routed to the doctor's office and returned within three days, possibly from a number he doesn't recognize. Great, so now he has to pick up the phone for an unfamiliar call from someone selling gutters or solar panels or some other useless product to see if it's his doctor.

Disgusted, he pops three cyclobenzaprine tablets, plops down and fades off to sleep. He will miss Lori's call two hours later and the doctor's office in three.

He wakes up at around four, sees the calls on his phone from Lori, Barry, and the doctor's office (it *is* a familiar number this time) and decides to call the office back first. To his amazement, someone answers the phone, knows who he is and says there was a cancellation next Friday at two and he can take his blood tests on Tuesday, without an appointment. He readily agrees and starts to dial Lori, still in a bit of a fog, when he hears tires screeching in his driveway. He looks out the window and sees a Mercedes SUV come to a stop within what looks like inches of his garage door.

There is pounding on the door and the doorbell repeatedly being rung and as Steve opens the door, his son is inches from his face, yelling at him. "Dad, what the hell is going on? Where were you? You don't show up to the game, you don't answer the phone. What the hell happened?"

"Calm down, please Barry. I was in pain and took some pills and fell asleep, that's all. I didn't hear the phone. I, I just got up."

"I'll say. You look like hell. Lori said you had pain in your arm. We thought you had a heart attack or something. Don't ever do that again. I ought to go through your medicine cabinet and get rid of whatever the fuck you took." Steve is almost shaking. Barry can yell, but he hardly ever swears. What have I done? That is all Steve can think.

"I'm sorry. I couldn't reach the doctor at first and I got frustrated and just took a few pills. Again, I apologize. I just talked to the doctor's office. They're getting me in late next week and I started to call Lori and you when I heard a car pull up. I'm okay, really."

Barry looks at him, hard, like he doesn't believe him. "I'm sorry I yelled but I think we have to start checking up on you more often."

Actually, Steve wasn't going to argue with that, at least not from his son. "Come on in. Want something cold?"

They sat and talked for a bit. Noel's team won. He got two hits, almost three, but the outfielder made a great catch at the fence. Barry asks about his weekend plans, and Steve tells him about his date with Candace. Normally Barry would be looking at the time, but Steve senses he was sticking around a bit longer than usual. He heard about Candace from Lori, and he seems really happy for Steve.

He finally gets up and Steve walks him to the door. Steve grabs him and turns him around and hugs him. "I love you, son."

"Me too, Dad, but please, don't do this again."

"I won't, I promise."

"Okay, have a great time tomorrow night. Let us know how it goes."

Steve laughs. "Your sister will know before I do."

Barry makes the connection. "Oh yeah, right, right," as he laughs too.

It's five-thirty and as Barry leaves, Steve realizes he can still catch the news with David Muir but then he curses because he realizes he hasn't called Lori back yet. Kids.

After the call, which went remarkably well, he pops a Healthy Choice meal in the microwave that he was going to eat for lunch. He then mixes Bombay Sapphire Gin with a small splash of diet tonic water and a piece of lime in a bar glass and watches the news. He flips to The History Channel, which usually has very little to do with history. After a second gin and tonic, he eats the Healthy Choice and some low carb-low sugar ice cream out of the carton and decides to take a walk, slipping into a pair of Skechers. The cool spring air feels good, but he soon tires and returns home.

After finishing his Stephen King novel, he watches a few minutes of the ten o'clock news and decides to go to bed. He'll have to shop tomorrow, off by two days now.

He has a very vivid dream about looking for Barry and Lori in a huge warehouse where he himself is lost. He has something important to tell Barry, but when he finally finds him and tries to talk to him, he turns away.

Steve suddenly wakes up and is breathing rapidly. He looks around a room that is unfamiliar to him. No gray curtains with tan horizontal shades. The bathroom isn't where it's supposed to be. And then he turns to his left and looks at the other side of the bed. No one is there, no Becky.

His arms and legs hurt. He realizes it is the present and that he is old. That life from even just almost a year ago has totally changed. He can't do certain things anymore like run or stay up late. He doesn't organize or attend charitable events anymore. Doesn't go to any activities at his temple anymore. Doesn't see that many people anymore except on Wednesday evenings and Sunday golf dates. He knows that his world has shrunk but the worst thing, more terrifying than any nightmare or Stephen King novel, is that he is alone and may be for the rest of his days.

Maybe those pills were an unconscious cry for attention.

He gets up from the bed and walks into the kitchen for some water and looks at the calendar on the refrigerator door for June with sparse dates filled in. He can remember a time when he had a diary book that would easily have twenty items a day. What has happened to him? Do things have to stay the way they are? No, except for his inherited health, he decides he can do something about it all, he can change.

"With God's help," he mutters.

CHAPTER FIFTEEN

S teve's phone rings the next morning at ten o'clock. He sees a Las Vegas number. "Hello?"

"Hi little brother, it's me. I got some news for you."

"Yeah Peter, what's up?"

"Well, I felt okay enough to stop by the dealership yesterday morning and guess what? The check was marked from a special account, but I had it traced back by the routing number and account number to Chase National Bank in Chicago, the account holder being one Danny Caruso. We got lucky, couldn't believe he wouldn't have used a bank check or draft, but now it makes sense because they didn't know the final amount with the sales tax."

"But Peter, didn't Johnny Rossi sign the check? How does that happen if it's Danny Russo's account? I don't get that part."

"I didn't get it either, but I had an investigator I know, who owes me a couple of favors, check out the account. And it turns out that Danny added Johnny as an additional signatory to the account a few days before he came out to Vegas and bought the car. My partner knew Johnny. Johnny used to work for him, and he must have somehow got proof of funds on the account otherwise the sale wouldn't have gone through. And get this, the bill of sale has it being shipped to the Wentworth address like I said, but Johnny Rossi used some address in Elmwood Park as his residence."

"Wow, well, what do we do now? I mean, your partner would be dragged into this and your dealership. Do you really want all that?"

"Look," Peter says. "You and I are three times seven. We know the FBI and Illinois cops have already interviewed Danny and probably suspect him. It's just a matter of time before the trail on the Dodge leads back here. I'm concerned about what *our* involvement would be if we handed over this info, not anything else. For instance, if we gave the FBI this information, would it mean we have to testify as to how we knew about all this, how we got it?"

"But how would we know that, Peter, if we didn't talk to them first?"

"Look, I know a retired FBI agent and I'm going to call him. No names, no specific facts, just what his opinion would be with this set of circumstances. Assuming I reach him today, I'll get back to you."

"I leave it in your hands, big brother, just let me know."

"I will, just hang tight."

When they clicked off, Steve sits for a while. His whole life, he has mostly ridiculed everything his brother has ever done. And now he seems to have found an incredible respect for him. How he's handling this situation, level-headed and serious with no levity or bravado. This is someone I suddenly admire, respect even, Steve thinks. After all these years. Whatever happens, I should see him more. Life is too damn short now.

Steve was going to call someone for lunch but puts that on hold in anticipation of a call back from Peter, even though he doesn't know when that will happen. He doesn't have to wait long because a half hour later his phone rings again, while listening to *Old Days* by Chicago, a song for some reason he gets teary-eyed every time he hears it.

"Steve, okay. This case is apparently huge because my friend, even though recently retired, knew about it. He was the go-to-guy in an organized task force against the Chicago Outfit for many years."

"You mean he was in Chicago?" Steve asks.

"Yes," Peter replies, "he retired out here. I sold him a car, and we became friends."

"Of course you did." Steve smiles and shakes his head.

"He tells me they have an old Outfit guy who they're going to indict on some old murder charges and they are going to make a plea deal with him, put the squeeze on him, *if* he agrees to meet Danny Caruso and wears a wire and Danny talks, incriminating himself. Then the evidence we give them can be used without us having to corroborate it, in other words to testify, although they will probably want affidavits. See, they wouldn't need what we have then."

"Oh wow. I can't believe it. So what's next?"

"They set up a meeting with us in the Vegas office. They tell us when and you get on a plane and get back out here. Save the ticket receipts because you'll be reimbursed. Wait for my call. He's putting everything in motion now. This case is very hot."

"Yeah, sure Peter. And Peter."

"What Stevie?"

"Great job, that's what. You really handled this well."

"We'll see. So far, so good."

"Right, sure."

Steve still can't believe what he just heard. He gets dressed and his head is swirling. Talking to the FBI, his brother taking the lead on something important, keeping Mike at bay, he can never know. And the family and everyone in the community, can they ever know? And what if these mob guys ever find out? Would they come after him, after Peter? Peter didn't seem scared about calling his FBI friend, is he not worried?

Steve puts on running shoes and decides to take a walk. He walks at a faster pace than usual down to Lake Cook Road and feels okay so he goes a bit further until he starts to feel tired, then turns around. When he gets back he showers, making sure his phone is in the bathroom.

The phone rings while he's still in his underwear. Potential spam. But as he goes into his closet for a shirt and pants, it rings again. Vegas.

"Hey, can you fly out here tomorrow morning? Got a tentative meeting with the feds at two o'clock your time if you can make it?"

"Yeah, I guess. I'll check now."

"Good. Listen little brother, I'm taking the heat on this. We started to talk about what was happening back home and we both knew Jack Heller. It's public knowledge that a neighbor witness saw a yellow sports car speed away. You mentioned it and the entire matter came up. I'll take it from there."

"Peter, I appreciate that but let me ask you something."

"Sure, what?"

"Aren't you a little bit, uh apprehensive as to the testimony and what might happen if it gets back to some people who may hold a grudge about this, like the grudge Danny Caruso had against Jack?"

"Naa, what do you think, I'm going to run scared? I've lived a full life and Jack Heller did me a solid. And if things work out our testimony, affidavits, whatever will be sealed. So the answer is no. Your testimony is only like an introduction so no worries there. But Mike can never know and I'm going to tell them that."

Steve sat back in his chair and sighed after they hung up and shook his head. A week ago his life seemed so mundane, so predictable. Now it seemed everything had changed. How is this possible and will it turn out well?

CHAPTER SIXTEEN

Steve finds flights on United for tomorrow and as soon as they're booked, calls Tony, hoping and praying he's open tomorrow morning. He is and can pick him up to go to the airport, but has a business class he's taking at Harper College in the evening. Of course, he has a friend who can possibly make the pick-up in the evening and will give Steve the number. He texts Peter the flight number and tells him he'll text him when he lands. Despite it being around one o'clock, Steve isn't hungry. He's got a New York strip steak defrosting to put on the grill for dinner and just has an avocado spread on crackers and a diet Arizona Iced Tea.

Even with everything swirling around him, he is still tired after lunch and sets his phone alarm to ring in three hours. Thankfully, the phone doesn't ring and as he gets up, he realizes he is very hungry. He lights the grill and goes back in the house to snap on the local five o'clock news. A story on the Heller murder comes on, indicating that even though Sheila and Nathan have been officially charged, law enforcement is looking into organized crime and that the FBI has fully taken over the investigation from local authorities. Steve thinks this is a good development, as it takes Mike out of the loop. Steve also realizes that aside from Peter and the FBI, he will tell no one, ever, about meeting with them. He is again convinced no good can come from mentioning it.

Dinner and the evening are uneventful. He has to find a

suit and tie to put on for the meeting tomorrow, something he has done only once or twice since Becky's funeral. He finds a blue Ralph Lauren suit and thin Zegna tie and tries on the suit to make sure it still fits, which it does. A long-sleeve button down blue poplin shirt completes the ensemble. He will watch a rerun of Ken Burn's documentary about Vietnam, the current episode dealing with 1968, a year he remembers well.

He sleeps surprisingly well and has a full breakfast, then gets dressed. After wearing a suit for so many years and then stopping for just a couple, it feels funny getting dressed up, tying a half Windsor tie and standing in front of a mirror. The only thing lacking is his former briefcase, but now he has no paperwork, just his E-tickets printed from the computer and his Kindle. Tony honks and they're on the way to O'Hare.

Steve had told Tony on his first Vegas trip that he was seeing his brother in the hospital and Tony asks if he was seeing him again and if he's okay. Steve replies that he is and that he's out of the hospital, this being a trip to see him on business. Tony spends the rest of the way complaining about how his daughter is being passed over for a promotion at work. Tony gives him the phone number of his friend for the return flight, and they wish each other well.

After clearing security and the long pedway ride, Steve finds his gate, but better yet, a Starbucks for a chai latte. He settles in to read Holly, another Stephen King novel, on his Kindle. As boarding time nears, he wisely uses the restroom and gets in line to board. There are a couple of men in sports coats, one with jeans, but it is safe to say he is the only one on the plane in a suit. Damn, he thinks, am I that old?

He has an aisle seat next to a young lady, who, from what he can see, appears to be taking an on-line course on her laptop. Do people read books anymore, especially students? Well, look at you, you've had your Kindle since Becky got it for you some fifteen years ago. He reads Stephen King's book until they serve snacks and drinks, then sleeps most of the rest of the way.

After finding a gate to the outside of the airport, he calls Peter, who says he will be by in about ten minutes, and to look for a white Audi sedan. Sure enough, the car pulls up with Peter in the passenger seat and another guy driving. Steve gets in the back.

"Hey little brother, how are you? This is Raul, he works for the dealership. He's gonna drop us off and pick us up from the FBI office."

Raul is dark, with wavy hair and a neat mustache. He waves to Steve as he pulls away.

"Hey Peter, hi Raul."

"You have a good flight? Nice suit."

"Yeah, uneventful."

"Well, here's the plan. We're going to give our statements and then they'll ask some questions. You're up first. We'll talk about how we both knew Jack, and both knew about the murder and how the neighbor saw the yellow car and they suspect Shiela and their son plus the Chicago Outfit. Then how I mentioned about the sale of the car. That's it. Don't bring Mike up and your little Wednesday night murder club. I'm sure they will, anyway. They know you guys are tight. Believe me, they've checked us both out backwards and forward."

Steve notices Peter has on a blue, muted plaid sports coat and a nice tie. "Okay. But Peter, I don't know about you, but I'm not telling *anyone* about this trip. No family, even immediate, no friends, no one."

"I understand Steve, I'll probably do the same, but it's nothing really to be ashamed of. Anyway, it's not going to help my business, so why would I? It's just going to lead to tons of unwanted publicity that we sold the car of a murderer."

"That's exactly my point," Steve answers. "Lots of publicity, most of it unwanted."

"Okay, so that's settled. Listen, these FBI people will not want us to say anything in any event. We have about another twenty minutes or so. There will be three people at the meeting. My retired friend, Elmer Houston, and he tells me two other agents. We're to go to the second floor but ask for Agent Craig Collins. when we get there. I've got copies of the check and bill of sale."

"This thing is just so surreal to me." Steve shakes his head. "I'm in a dream."

"Kind of jolted out of your quiet, routine retired life, huh?" Peter smiles.

"Yeah, you could say that."

The car finally pulls up to 1787 Lake Mead Boulevard, a long, low-slung building with a rather short, innocuous looking iron fence running across the front. They enter and are met by two young men, probably in their thirties, at a desk. Peter announces who they are and that they're here to see Agent Collins on the second floor and one man picks up a phone and apparently reaches Agent Collins. After nodding, the man asks for ID cards and looks at their driver's licenses for a minute and asks Peter and Steve to step on the side of the desk while the other man searches them with an electronic wand. When finished, the other man hands them lanyards with visitor tags that they put around their necks along with their licenses and tells them to take the elevator to room 207. They approach waist-high glass gates running before and across the elevators, which open as they step in front of them.

Room 207 is a conference room with an all-glass front, which they enter. Agent Collins greets them at the door. He is in his late forties, Asian, with short, cropped hair turning gray at the temples. He introduces them to the other agent, Diedre Hall,

African American and younger, mid-thirties and very attractive, especially in a dark tailored blue business suit. The third person is Elmer Houston, a large, burly man with a magnificent head of gray hair and mustache to match. Elmer and Peter exchange pleasantries asking about health and family, then everyone is seated, Peter and Steve on one side of a wood conference table with the other three on the other side.

Agent Collins tells everyone the meeting was about to begin and is being recorded as Agent Hall presses a button on a triangular device in the middle of the table. Collins then states who is at the meeting and the purpose, to provide additional information regarding the death of one Jack Heller.

Steve starts, telling who he is, where he lives, former occupation, etc. He then states how he was in Peter's hospital room when the subject of the Heller murder came up and he mentioned that a neighbor saw a yellow car speeding away from Heller's driveway after she heard shots and they discussed the make and that Nathan Heller's car was a Camaro. That led to how Peter's dealership sold a yellow Dodge Charger RT to someone in Chicago, which turned out to be Johnny Rossi. Peter later traced it to Chicago and to Johnny Rossi's address, then traced the check to Danny Caruso, but how Rossi was added as a signatory a few days before the purchase and why Peter thought that was done.

They only had a few questions for him. Collins asked if he knew Jack Heller personally and then Hall asked about Mike Baricello. They obviously knew that they were friends with each other, just as Peter had said. She asked if Mike and he had discussed the case and Steve admitted that they had and how Steve told Mike he thought Heller's wife and son were being framed. Collins and Hall made a few notes, and that was it for Steve.

Peter's statement and questions went a bit longer, but there were no surprises. When it was over, Collins told them what Peter already knew and had told Steve, that they were closing in on Danny. Someone was meeting him while wearing an audio and visual wire and if successful he would incriminate himself and that would be the 'nail in the coffin' as Collins put it, the only loose end possibly being where Johhny Rossi or his body is. Collins concluded by asking Peter and Steve to say nothing about this meeting or what they knew, at least until the case was closed. Both Peter and Steve readily agreed.

And that was it. It took about an hour and as they left, Collins simply reminded them to drop off their visitor badges at the front desk. Before the elevator takes them downstairs, Peter has called Raul to come pick them up.

"That wasn't too bad," Peter says. "We're clearly a side show if the wire evidence comes through."

"But Peter, if it doesn't, we made the case. Your documents with the car and the bank account are solid proof, no matter what."

"I know, but let's hope it doesn't come to that."
Steve just nods.

CHAPTER SEVENTEEN

anny Caruso is sitting in a booth at Lou Mitchell's Restaurant on West Jackson Boulevard flipping through the Sun Times newspaper. He's in his early fifties with slick black hair and dark skin, wearing a black Armani shirt and Gucci loafers and a gold chain with a small gold horn hanging just below his neckline. Danny is a truck dispatcher for a large trucking company that has its operations terminal in the southeast Chicago neighborhood of Hegewisch, with offices in Chicago's Chinatown area off of 26th Street. In reality, he is a mid-level capo or captain of the Chicago Outfit, the city's organized crime organization. He is part of what's known as the Chinatown Crew, headed by his father, Mike Caruso, formerly headed by his uncle and dad's brother, David Caruso. David Caruso is doing twenty years in the Atlanta Federal Penitentiary, while Mike Caruso was found to be not guilty of the same offenses.

The Caruso brothers were tried at the same time and represented by the same lawyer, Jack Heller. It was the same charges, RICO and illegal gambling operations, strong-arming bars to put in video poker machines, loan sharking and money laundering. To Danny and many other people, it seemed like the same case. It was Heller's idea to try them together, and the brothers agreed with the strategy. But the jury didn't think so.

After the trial, Danny paid a visit to Heller's office. He

received an icy reception and found Heller to be pompous and arrogant, stating he was confident that on appeal (probably at least two years down the road), his uncle's conviction would be overturned. But he left the office with a sour taste in his mouth, as if he were belittled. Danny was a hothead and had been arrested three times in five years for assault, but was never convicted.

His dad, known to be a reasonable and mild-mannered fellow for a mobster, had talked to Heller by phone, asking the same questions. Mike Caruso complained to his son as well, that Heller was very dismissive and yelling at Mike, "Didn't you get what you paid for?" That did it for Danny. On that day, months ago, he decided to have Jack Heller 'whacked' as the term goes.

Danny and a couple of Outfit 'soldiers' found out where Jack lived, but more importantly, where his ex-wife and son lived. He had heard that their divorce had been downright nasty and took to the idea of framing them by planting evidence. But who to do the big deed itself? Enter Johnny Rossi, a soldier of the Chinatown Crew who had been to jail twice for robbery and arson, owed his ex-wife more money than he'd ever make and had a job as a truck driver for the same Outfit freight company. In short, someone who needed money and was desperate.

Rossi would receive ten grand in cash and was told to buy a car to match Heller's son Nathan's 2023 yellow Chevy Camaro. He was also told a dealer in Vegas that the Outfit had used could get that car. So Rossi was paid, bought the car and on a Tuesday night months later gunned down Heller in his driveway. He then met Danny Caruso in a parking lot behind a small restaurant in Elmwood Park and gave him the gun. Rossi was almost proud of the hit, saying it went off without a hitch. But Danny looked at the car and asked why it was a Camaro, not a Dodge Charger? A huge argument ensued, Rossi insisting Danny said get a Camaro and Danny went nuts. The argument got so heated, he pulled out a thirty-eight-caliber revolver from his waist and shot Rossi three times in the head. Since they were in Danny's car already, he just closed the door, lowered the body, and drove away. The body would later end up in the back of a truck owned by Juarez Trucking in Cicero, but this was only temporary.

Today at the restaurant he is waiting for an old Outfit guy, semi-retired, named Sal DiMucci. Sal came in and Danny waved him over to his booth in the back. Sal is late 70s, bald and overweight, wearing what looks to be a bowling shirt but without his name on it. He had gone to jail years ago for heading the numbers racket for the Outfit's Chicago Heights Crew, and also for attempted murder. The thing that Sal was known for, however, was permanently disposing of bodies. He was a master at it and although it didn't come up that frequently, he was the man to call when it did. Like now.

They exchange pleasantries and order breakfast. Danny gets a jardiniere omelet and Sal the Belgium malted waffle. Danny goes into great detail about what happened and how after he killed Rossi he went up to Sheila Heller's condo, broke into her car and slipped a note in the glove box with Johnny Rossi's name and number, covering his face and hands with a skin darkening cream and wearing a hoodie so if there were cameras in the garage they would think he was a Black guy, then going outside, breaking into Nathan's Camaro and putting the gun in his trunk.

Sal keeps nodding, saying little except asking if his dad, Mike, knew all this.

"He does now," Danny laughs. "He don't care. He thought Heller was an asshole and, from what he says, anyone can handle the appeal at this point."

Sal nods again and asks where the body is when their food suddenly arrives. They switch to talking about family, personal things, now keeping away from business, and after the plates are cleared, Danny slips him the address of where the truck is in Cicero. Sal simply says "okay" and they get up to leave. When they're outside, he asks. "I get the deal with planting the gun, but why the note?"

"Aww, that's just to throw the cops off and maybe add to the frame up theory. To tell you the truth, Sal, I was just havin' a little fun."

"Oh," replies Sal, and they shake hands and walk away in opposite directions.

CHAPTER EIGHTEEN

Saturday morning finds Steve shopping at Jewel in Glenview, getting essentials he forgot at Mariano's. His arm and back seem okay, but he still feels awfully tired from the latest Vegas trip. He arrived home late yesterday after Tony's friend picked him up at the airport.

The cashier asks if he needs help to his car with his substantial load of groceries and he says yes. He pulls the big SUV up to the loading area and marvels as some teen-age kid swings his groceries into the back when the hatch opens, almost effortlessly. Steve is sure it will not be that easy taking them out when he's home. He makes a stop at Binny's Beverage Depot. It's out of his way, but he has an account there and he'll ask about a good red and white wine to bring. Candace still hasn't called him, which means she hasn't made up her mind about what to make for dinner, although he thought she was leaning towards seafood.

After coming home and bringing all the groceries in she does call, but dinner is not the first thing on her mind. "Hi Steve, it's Candace. I heard you weren't well."

Oh shit, Steve thinks. This is Lori's doing. "No, I had some back and arm pain and made a mistake by taking one too many muscle relaxers, that's all. I'm fine now."

"Are you sure? Because we can postpone this. I'm making

poached salmon but haven't put it in the oven yet."

"No, I'm fine, really. That sounds great. I'm bringing a great wine for seafood, a chardonnay. I have a red too if we were having chicken or meat."

She laughs, that titter. "Oh my, should I put a steak in as well?"

He laughs. "I'm sure whatever you're making will be great. What time should I be there?"

"Is five-thirty too early? I want you to find a place to park without too much of a hassle. There's a bank parking lot behind my building, just go around the block. At five-thirty, there should be some spaces there."

"Sounds good. Anything else I can bring besides the wine?"

"Just your company. You sure you're feeling okay?"

"I will be once I see you." He sort of lowers his voice. Did I really say that? He thinks?

"Aww, flattery will get you somewhere." She titters again.

Annoying, but I can get used to it. He smiles. "Okay, see you then."

"See ya Steve."

All of a sudden, he panics when he turns off his phone. He grabs for his date calendar book on the kitchen counter and finds the date for this past Thursday. He thought his grandson Randy had a baseball game that he possibly missed. He told his daughter-in-law Michelle that he'd be there. Thankfully, it's next Thursday, and he utters a prayer of thanks. With all this Vegas stuff going on, he's surprised he hasn't forgotten a lot of things.

He calls a Sunday golfing buddy, Ned Langer. who's having hip surgery next week so he can get the details and see him at

Evanston Hospital. He then calls Peter but gets no answer, so he leaves word. Then Lori calls and he sighs and lets it go to voice mail. "Hi Daddy, just checking up on you and wondering if you're still going out tonight with Candace and to remind you Noel has a first playoff game tomorrow at the field on Techny at eleven, although it's supposed to rain. I'll remind you again. If you go out, have fun and be nice."

Steve just rolls his eyes and shakes his head. He is still in the kitchen and starts to look at a pile of saved mail. The Westfield Chamber of Commerce is having a carnival and raffle coming up. They have left him alone since Becky passed, but maybe it's time to call Mike Duffy and volunteer again. Then he picks up a temple bulletin. The Men's Club has its annual barbecue in the last week in June and it's the temple's annual meeting the next night. He and Becky were both active as past board members and he was once president of the congregation years ago. Again, people gave him space after she died. No one called about committee meetings or the golf outing this July. Maybe it's time to get your ass in gear, Steve.

He flips through more brochures and flyers, for a blood drive, park district movie nights and classes, more charities and fourth of July activities for the village which he used to be involved with. Then he yawns, repeatedly. He silences his phone and sets the timer on it for ninety minutes. Why am I always so damned tired? And then he wraps a pillow around his head and curls up on the couch and is asleep within minutes. When the alarm on his phone goes off, Steve feels rested. He sees there are two calls, from Peter then Lori.

"Hey little brother. I'm still at home and feeling better, getting some TLC from Amy. Quite a meeting, huh? I'll call you as soon as I hear anything. Should be soon. Take care."

Then Lori. "Hi Dad. Just an FYI, Noel's game is at the Techny field on Sunday at eleven if it doesn't rain. Oh, I know you probably have golf then, but you'll probably play even if it's a downpour. Anyway, remember I'm bringing in pizza tomorrow night and Barry's gang is coming. Don't forget. Oh, and have fun tonight. Remember to be nice and listen. Bye."

Steve just sighs. He remembers how he offered Lori money for the pizzas, and she got mad, but why should she spend a dime to get the family together? Barry should be doing that, or he should. Maybe he'll pull what his kids used to call 'The Kaufman Cash Shuffle.' Years back, when the kids were both first married, they would order in dinner at one of their houses and Steve would offer to pay. They refused, so he would leave money under a jar or inside a microwave. Then on the way home, he'd call them and tell them where it was.

The last time he did it, many years ago now, it was at Barry's last house. He left the money in the refrigerator in a vegetable bin. Becky didn't know, but when they were in the car and Steve called the house, she had an inkling of what was going on. When Steve told Barry where to look, Barry started to complain and was clearly annoyed. Steve asked him what he was complaining about because everyone likes 'cold cash.' He couldn't remember when Becky had laughed so long and hard, and even Barry chuckled. Steve pursed his lips and shuddered as he thought about this. What good times, he thought. Now all I have are memories. And it seems all my good memories have been made.

CHAPTER NINETEEN

With these thoughts still on his mind, Steve strips down and looks at himself in the mirror. He always had a full head of hair with curls at the end. He mostly still does, but it's all gray and his hairline goes back a way. His eyes have bags under them which he will try to rub out with some wrinkle cream after his shower.

After showering he puts on a button-down shirt, blue slacks and new Hokas. He makes sure the white wine is in the gift sleeve he bought. The heck with the red. He goes by the door to the garage to view his memory checklist, sets the alarm (Becky5) and gets in the Lincoln.

The ride is stress free, and he listens to the country station, but there are too many commercials, so he switches to classic rock. He spots the bank parking lot, which is about half full, but it's still only about five-ten. So, as with his first date with her, he stalls, listening to *Beast of Burden* by the Stones, followed by *Free Falling* by Tom Petty. Steve is crazy about Tom Petty and more so now that he's gone. He would listen to a Petty song all the way through even if it would make him late to something. It's five-twenty-one, and he calls her.

"Hi, how are you?" she almost sings. Steve again thinks she would sound this cheery if the apocalypse was here.

"I'm good. I'm in the bank lot, but how do I get to the front of your...."

"Oh, no worries. Just walk through the building parking lot and let me know when you're at the back door. I can buzz you in from the back. You walk down the hall to the lobby and take the elevator to the fourth floor. I'm in 402."

"Okay, give me a minute."

She buzzes him up, and it appears there are only about eight apartments on the floor. She is at the door wearing a solid purple silk blouse with dark slacks, a string of pearls, and matching earrings. He thinks she's overdressed if they were going out to a nice place, let alone for an evening at home. They kiss and embrace for a long time, and he whispers that he missed her, then thinks he may regret that as it's only been a week. She nods while they're embracing, so that's a good sign.

Candace shows him around the apartment, which is huge. Steve knows real estate, and he guesses it's about twenty-three hundred square feet. She has two huge bedrooms, each with a full bath and there's a powder room, a large living room and a separate dining room with a very long galley kitchen that ends in a square eating area. There is a long balcony with Western exposure and a very nice view. Then she has an office/exercise room. The apartment is elegantly furnished but not gaudy, with beautiful Brazilian Rosewood floors (he later learns) and Oriental rugs. There is very nice contemporary and beautifully framed artwork throughout. She asks him to sit on a velvet couch in the living room while she checks on the food. He asks if he can help but she waives him off.

She returns. "Well, everything is coming along nicely, maybe ten minutes or less." She puts both hands on her knees. "So how was your week?" she asks.

He tells her it was ordinary except for his day trip to Vegas to see Peter.

"Why didn't you stay longer?"

Steve is uncomfortable about this but tries to explain. "My brother is somewhat hard to take. It's always been that way between us. Even though he's older, he's kind of, kind of immature. Very impulsive and if things don't work out, there's always an excuse. Don't get me wrong, I love him, would do anything for him, *have* done a lot of things for him but, I don't know."

She puts her chin in her palm and looks into his eyes. "I know exactly what you mean. My younger sister, Marcy, is that way. I love her, have listened to her *tsuris*, helped her through things, but a day or two with her and I'm done. It's exhausting and really it's. What's the word I'm looking for?"

"In my case, it's annoying," Steve answers.

She claps her hands together and laughs. This time not just a titter. "Exactly, she's damn annoying!" They both laugh.

"I should open the wine," he says.

"Follow me. I'll get you a corkscrew to slice open the wrapper and open the bottle."

He does and thinks what if the bottle had a screw top, which he would never bring to someone's house, or at least not here, now?

She leads him to a huge drawer she opens, which is laid out like a surgical table. She finds the corkscrew and hands it to him. "I'm going to check on the salmon and garlic bread."

"Sounds good." He gets the wrapper off easy enough, but the corkscrew is proving difficult to turn once it's in and rotating. He puts the bottle in a sink for better leverage and hikes up his long sleeve shirt, preparing for the worst. But the corkscrew starts turning a bit easier now. She comes over by him and spots his watch. "That's beautiful, simple, but very elegant."

"Thanks. It was my dad's. He collected watches. Some he bought, others patients gave him as gifts."

"Oh, that's right. You mentioned in the restaurant that he saved a few patients' lives by detecting cancer in time for surgery."

"Yep, and a couple of them gave him watches as presents. Then he had a few passed down from his dad and he also bought more. This one's a Patek Philippe Calatrava. It's not their most expensive watch by far. They have watches worth millions of dollars, but I like it. It's over a hundred years old and it keeps great time. The company's motto is you never own one of their watches, you just keep it for the next generation. There we go." The cork is out.

"So will Barry get it?" she asks.

"I really don't know. You'd think he'd want the watches, but he doesn't wear them, doesn't appreciate them and mentioned if he had them, he might sell them. That hurt."

"Did you tell him that? I just find we've got to be honest with our kids."

"No, I gave him a dirty look, though. He knew what I was thinking."

"It would seem to me that unless you put it in your will or leave instructions about them, you'll have no say in it," she replies.

"No say? Why's that?"

"Because you'll be gone," she smiles wryly.

"Oh, very funny. I'm still thinking it through."

"Well, dinner's ready. I've got the glasses out there for wine and water."

They go into the dining room, and he pulls her chair out as

if they were dining out. The dining room table is easily ten feet long, but their seats are at one end, facing each other. There is a red tablecloth on their portion of the table with fine China dishes and her 'good' silver and napkins in brass holders.

He pours the wine and holds up his glass for a toast. "To our health and happiness." He wants to apologize. That sounded dumb.

"To us," she responds. That sounds better. He's relieved.

"Yes, to us," he adds back.

Dinner is great. The salmon is done to perfection, flaky and moist. They continue playing Jewish geography, which they did at the restaurant. It's hard because her dad was a jeweler in the Cleveland area and Steve grew up in West Ridge on Chicago's far North side. Candace Lerner went to college at the University of Wisconsin in Madison, where she met Chad Miller, and they married upon graduation. He was an accountant who worked for the IRS, then went into private practice with a big eight firm until he wanted to get into the jewelry business. Candace's father helped set him up. They had always lived in Highland Park and raised two girls, Linda, the therapist who knows Lori, and Audrey, a younger daughter who lives in Dallas and works for the Small Business Administration. Lori has seen Linda professionally many times, even though it doesn't seem very professional.

For dessert, she has cookies from Mariano's and a fruit bowl. He helps clear the table and they watch the nine o'clock news on WGN. He's holding her hand when he admires her watch, an Ebel with diamonds around the face, and she blushes a bit. "It's nice, a fortieth wedding anniversary gift, but it's not in your league."

"Oh, don't say that," he replies. "My favorite watch is one I got on an e-Bay auction. It's a Ball railroad watch certified to tell time by the railroads for use by conductors, engineers, brakemen, and it's a simple watch with big numbers and a canvas strap. It costs maybe six hundred bucks, but I love it. It's what you like that counts, not the cost."

She looks at him and smiles. "You are a wise man, Mr. Kaufman, a very wise and thoughtful guy."

"Why thank you Mrs. Miller. I appreciate that."

They talk on. She's playing tennis tomorrow; he's playing golf and having dinner at his daughter's. It turns out she is as well. They talk about their relationship with their kids, how it's hard not to interfere with what they see, worried about being a burden as they get older. They both agree that their kids and families have their own lives to live and that parents are along for the ride. "It's not our ride anymore," Steve says. She nods, sniffs a bit.

What Steve wants to say is that he's lonely. That's the worst thing for him, that's what he wants to change. But he feels that he dare not mention this because what if she's not? What if she's really happy, like lots of unattached women and men, perfectly happy to exist alone in the world seeing friends and family once in a while? And if she is happy right now, then he comes off being needy, being vulnerable, weak even? No, he thinks, let sleeping dogs lay. Maybe another time.

The news is typical. It starts out with a shooting, then some political news, followed up by a human-interest story or two, the weather and sports. They discuss who they each look like, and she goes into her bedroom and takes out a photo album and goes through it with him. His arm is around her. Her mother was very pretty, and Candace has her face and eyes, except for her nose, which is long but thin, like her dad's.

He starts to yawn, then she does, and she says he made her do it. They laugh and he says he should probably get going. He has an early tee time at Ivanhoe and it's not that close. She agrees.

He embraces her and says he had a wonderful time and that she's a great cook, again praising the salmon. He goes on to say he has no dating experience but that he's not just feeding her a line, telling her what a lady wants to hear. He says he's just being sincere.

She says she knows that and that he's a great guy. He's genuine and is sincere, a true gentleman and everything in between. She goes on to say she hasn't been on that many dates, but enough to know that he is special to her. He appreciates that and that he'll call her early in the week. They kiss and she asks if he'll text when he gets home. He says, "Yes Mom," and she punches him lightly in the arm. He figures he'll really know how the date went tomorrow night at his daughter's house.

CHAPTER TWENTY

He almost sleeps through his alarm that is going off, but after about ten minutes he gets up and ultimately out of bed. Thank goodness his arm and shoulder don't hurt, and he just has a small pain in his back in one spot. Some lidocaine will cover that. He grabs a bagel and coffee, downing vitamins with it, then gets dressed and heads for the golf course, but his mind isn't on golf. It's on last night. What's going to happen? Where is this headed? She's so nice, almost too nice. And she's pretty. Sure, she has some crow's feet and lines she conceals, but hell, she's seventy-three going on seventy-four in July and she looks damn good to me or anyone else.

Golf had mixed results. Steve's drives were always good. His long, lanky frame was made for golf. His short game today, not so much. One of his golfing buddies had a sister who never married, and she was in town from Del Ray Beach down Florida way. Roger had mentioned her before and showed Steve a picture of her on his phone more than once.

Roger was surprised when Steve begged off. Not because of what he thought Steve said, that it was still too soon for him to date, but that he *was* dating and thought it might be going some place. Steve hadn't mentioned this to anyone, but he realized after last night that he was, in fact, dating someone, and maybe he should mention it. Of course, he could be putting a curse on the whole situation by saying this too early. That's how a conservative, semi-neurotic ex-banker thinks.

As Steve gets into his car on this warm June day, he finds himself still sweating, even after a quick shower in the club's locker room area. And he is tired again. It seemed like an effort just to push the ignition button and hit the Lincoln's push button drive system.

When he arrives home, he changes, then finds a piece of rye bread to nibble on.

Then he calls Lori to confirm the time of six o'clock for dinner but really to get the scoop on last night. "Hi Lori? How are you-how was Noel's game?"

"Fine Daddy, he got two hits but then struck out on a bad pitch, so he's upset."

"Did you tell him every time he's at bat; it can't always be a hit?"

"I did, but he's upset with himself because it was a bad pitch."

"Oh, he'll get over it," Steve laughs. "Is it six tonight?"

"Yes, I think I'm going to Pizza Hut. They have a special and their crust is good. You think that's okay?"

"Sure, why not? How's Steph?"

"She's fine. She's going to a birthday party for a late lunch at that new Mexican restaurant on Skokie Boulevard."

"Right, right, right. Supposed to have good fajitas. And how are you?"

"Dad, I'm fine and you're fine too."

"Oh, I am?"

"Yes. Candace really likes you. I mean she really does."

"That's great honey, cause I really like her too. I'm just worried I'm going to do something to screw this up."

"No Dad, you're not. Just be yourself. It's working so far. She likes everything about you, even the way you walk."

"The way I walk. Wait, what?"

"You lope Dad. She thinks it's cute."

"I know I kind of do, but no one has ever said it's cute."

"Oh yes, they do. Mom used to think it was cute."

"She did? She never mentioned it to me."

"Girl talk, Dad, girl talk. Listen, I have to get Stephanie there. We're late."

"Okay, see ya later. Love you."

"Love you too."

She likes me a lot. Wow. That's good, isn't it? I would think so. He goes into the kitchen and makes himself a turkey sandwich on rye with hot mustard and a diet root beer. Then he goes into the office and looks up Steve Goldstein's number, the President of the temple's Men's Club. They haven't talked in a while and Goldstein is surprised to hear from him. Steve tells him he is going to call Jerry Lane and see if he can get in on a foursome for the golf outing and that he wants to sponsor something. Goldstein is excited and makes several suggestions, depending on what he wants to spend. Steve asks if he can be a lead sponsor for a grand and Steve Goldstein says absolutely and he's glad he's back.

Steve has Jerry Lane on speed dial. They've been friends for thirty years and Jerry was Steve's doctor before he retired. He gets his voicemail and asks if it's too late to be part of a foursome Jerry usually puts together for the outing.

Then Steve looks up Fred Cane's number, the head of the Westfield Chamber of Commerce. They have also been friends for years, but they've only talked a couple times since Becky passed. But Steve is suddenly very tired and goes into the bedroom. His back and arm start to ache, and he takes an Aleve but keeps away from the Cyclobenzaprine. He puts his phone on the nightstand and is out in minutes.

The phone wakes him up at around ten to five. It's Lori. "Daddy, something awful has happened!"

"What is it honey, what?"

"It's Stephanie. She was at the party and got violently ill, throwing up, headache, they called the paramedics who took her to Westbrook Hospital. I'm there now."

"Hold on, what do they think it is?"

"Someone in emergency thinks she has all the symptoms of food poisoning, but they don't know yet. I'm waiting to speak to a doctor. I'm here with Noel, we're waiting. I called Michelle. She and Barry were going to come by, but I said not to."

"Well, I'm coming. Listen honey, don't worry. It was probably something she ate there. I'll be there in a few." He hangs up.

Steve gets in the car and makes his way to the hospital in Glenview, an adjoining suburb to Westfield. He is obviously concerned about his granddaughter but is just as concerned that she's at Westbrook Hospital. What did Barry used to say about it when he was a lawyer? You can't sue them if they do something wrong because if you go there, you assume the risk. Yeah, that's it. Barry called it 'The Assumption of Risk Doctrine.'

And Barry was right. Steve remembers when his friend Al Diamond took his mother to Westbrook when she was having chest pains. They ran some tests and cleared her to go home, stating she had indigestion. The next day she had chest pains again while shopping with Al in Evanston. They were right near Evanston Hospital, so he took her there, again into emergency. They confirmed that she was having *another* cardiac episode, and that she had one the day before.

Steve, like many others, had long been concerned that Westbrook was the closest hospital in an emergency situation, even though they were now part of one of the hospital 'networks' as they were known. He finds a spot to park near the Emergency Room and tells a security guard that his daughter and granddaughter are in the waiting room, and he's waved through.

He easily spots Lori and Noel as they're the only ones in the waiting room. He hugs Lori, who is obviously a mess, and then Noel who is absorbed with some portable video game.

"What's the word?"

"A doctor came out once and said all the signs show food poisoning, but they're not finished with the tests and then they have to look at them. They gave her a sedative and inserted a tube to pump her stomach, if there was anything left in there." Lori gives a little smile.

"She's gonna be fine honey," Steve smiles back. "Just something that didn't agree with her. But I'd check with the other mothers you know who had girls there, see if they had any issues."

"Good idea Dad, I'll do that." Then she starts to sob. "Oh Daddy, I just wanted to get the family together, I, I'm so sorry."

He holds her again. "What do you have to be sorry about Lori? This is certainly not your fault. It's not anyone's fault except maybe the restaurant. It will all be fine. Why don't I take Noel, we'll get something to bring back to eat? You said it could still be awhile. Can we eat in here?"

"I think so, there was a family in here before. Their son was in a bad accident. They had Brown's Chicken with them. What would you get?"

"Pizza, what else?" He smiles. He puts his hand under her chin. "Dominos." They both smile. She nods.

"Come on buddy," he says to Noel who follows him out. He orders a large cheese and sausage from the car with some diet drinks. "Where do you guys eat after the games if you go out?" he asks Noel.

"A few times we ate at Barny's."

"You like it there?"

"Ahh, it's okay. Last time we had it I thought it was kinda greasy."

"Yes, that happened to me there when I was with a friend. I think they put too many toppings on it and didn't bake it through but you're right, it was kind of greasy. So, how's baseball going? I hear you were upset for swinging at a bad pitch."

"I am Papa. It was way outside. I should have waited. Uncle Barry said I should be aggressive and step into the ball but to also wait for your pitch. Problem was, I couldn't wait for a decent pitch cause this guy was throwing wild. None of his pitches were good, although we did win and are in the semis of the playoffs."

"Great, but Mom also said you got two hits earlier."

"Different pitcher. First one was getting rocked," Noel replies.

"Oh, I get it. But Uncle Barry's right. Usually, you wait for a good pitch."

"Yeah, I know. Papa, did you teach Uncle Barry how to play baseball?"

Steve ponders this for a bit. "I did, but he had a lot of practice with our next-door neighbor, an older boy who was really good. I don't know where he found the time, but he did. I mean, I would practice with him, but he learned an awful lot, probably when he was younger than you. I was working a lot of hours up until Uncle Barry was about your age. It's not an excuse, but it's just the way things were." After all these years Steve has trouble with that question. He always wonders if maybe he wasn't around enough for Barry and that there's resentment towards him for it.

"No, I get it. Papa, can I ask you something else?"

"Sure sport, what is it?"

"I was with my friend Taren, and he said Coach Graff said something about you."

"About me? Uh oh," Steve says.

"No, it's okay. Coach Graff said you were one of the best liked people in the community. Why would he say that? Were you a hero or something?" Noel looks at him with wide eyes and a curious look.

Steve laughs. "No, I do know coach Graff's parents, they're old friends and customers of the bank and I watched Gordy, err Coach Graf growing up. I think he meant that I just know lots of people in the area, from work and from charity work that I did with Nana years ago. Yep, I think that's what he meant."

"I still think that's pretty cool though," Noel says.

Just then Lori calls.

"We're just here Lori, walking into the store."

"Okay, but change of plans. Stephanie was just released. She has to rest now, and I'll have to get her a prescription for her stomach in the morning, but we're done. I'm going to drive home. Can you just come there with the food?"

"Of course, I was going to get drinks with the food."

"No need, I just bought a load of drinks and Stephanie can

have a Seven-Up. That will be her dinner."

"Okay, got it." He goes in with Noel and stands behind him and gives Noel his credit card and tells him to ask for a pickup for Kaufman. Noel beams with pride that he will pay for the food which was the idea.

Steve stays at Lori's until about eight-thirty and goes home. He reads a bit and struggles to try to stay up to catch John Oliver's show but can't keep his eyes focused for the last fifteen minutes and goes to bed thinking about what guns he's going to shoot with at the range tomorrow morning and thinks about Candace. Are these somehow psychologically related?

CHAPTER TWENTY-ONE

Steve is coming back from Gat Guns in East Dundee and is pleased with himself. The last time he went to the range he had trouble steadying his Smith & Wesson 686-6 revolver from the recoil. His wrists seemed to be weakened, so he went to Dick's Sporting Goods and bought an adjustable hand grip and has been using it. It seemed to help, and his aim improved without the recoil of the gun to ruin his shots. He had told Candace on their first date that he owns handguns, has a concealed carry permit, and shoots.

She simply said "Oh," and then somehow the subject was changed.

He hopes it won't be an issue but thinks, 'What if she asks me to stop? What would I say, do?' Then he thinks this is silly, he's getting way ahead of things. But then he thinks, 'What if we moved in together and she asks me, saying she can't have guns in the house?' Holy crap, what am I thinking! The phone rings in the car, breaking up his train of thought.

"Steve?"

He doesn't recognize the number. "Yes?"

"Fred Cane. How are you? Steve the man!"

"Hey Fred, how are you doing?"

"How are *you* doing my friend, that's the question? It's been a long time."

"Yes, it has. I've taken my time but I'm slowly returning to things. I think I'd like to get involved with the Chamber again if you can use an old, retired banker who's a bit cantankerous."

"Steve, we can always use *you*. Heck, we'd create something for you to do."

They both laugh at that.

"Well, have you got anything coming up?" Steve asks.

"Sure do, we've got committees for the Fourth of July parade and gathering at Village Green. You know everyone on the Board, Artie, Nick, Singh and Dave Ryan. If I tell them you want to get involved they'd probably want you to run the whole shebang!"

Steve responds, still laughing, "Fred, I don't want to put you out of a job, I'm just looking to help out, for something to do."

"I know Steve, just a little levity, probably very little. It's just so good to hear from you!"

"The same here Fred, it's mutual. We always worked well together."

"Tell you what, check what you're doing a week from today at lunch. The Board usually meets at a restaurant in addition to the usual bimonthly meetings on Tuesday nights. We'd love to see you there. Your email hasn't changed, has it?"

"Nope. That sounds great."

"Good, hold it open. I gotta run, got somebody coming into the office shortly. I'm still working a few days a week."

"Great, I'll look for an email. Take care."

"You too pal. Did I say it's great hearing from you?" He starts to laugh again.

"Several times Fred." Steve's jaw tightens. Yes, I've served my time and can tell anyone I've earned the right to walk away but I still enjoy this, I need to have purpose in my life and I'm far from done. God knows, if this keeps up, I may even reopen my Facebook account.

When he reaches home, he changes and calls Evanston Hospital to see how Ned Langer is. When he's connected to his room his wife, Marsha, answers. She says he's doing fine. The fusion went well but he's going to be there a couple more days, probably out on Wednesday. She said he'd love to see him when he asks.

Steve takes the Edens down to Skokie to reach Evanston Hospital but stops first at a Burger King for his favorite, two honey mustard wraps. He won't eat in the car. Not because he might make a mess as he'd use a stack of paper napkins but because the food would leave a smell in his precious car. He realizes this is stupid because over three weeks' time the only people in his car have been Candace twice and Noel. But you can't change the spots on a leopard or the habits of people, especially in their golden years.

Ned brightens when he sees Steve. He has a gravelly voice and was a general counsel for a big insurance company. Of course they talk about golf. Steve has an eight handicap and Ned has a seven. Ned is as animated as he can be with a brace around his mid-section.

Steve leaves to return home. He's going to call Candace tonight and is uncertain about what to say as to where a third date should be. Another restaurant, movie, last minute try for a play? She did say she's not a fan of going down in the city, thank goodness. Steve tries to avoid that like the plague. It is a beautiful town. The skyline is magnificent, and the weather is nice. But with the traffic everywhere, lack of parking, crime, it's just a turn off. And it's for the young.

He comes home and goes down to his basement to practice some golf shots into a net he has rigged up, using a wedge, then practices putting into an electric retrievable golf hole device in another part of the basement. Dinner is already predetermined. It's leftover pizza from last night as Lori only ate one slice and Noel less than that. He'll make a salad to add to it.

His phone rings and he sees it's Peter. "What's up Peter."

"Got some news little brother. Elmer called me and said they have the whole confession from Danny on video He sang like a bird. His attorneys came into the Chicago FBI office and watched it. Then they told them if there was any doubt, they have sworn statements and documents showing Rossi bought the Dodge Charger out of Caruso's account. It's over. He's going to try and take a plea but doesn't have much to work with. We're done but still don't say anything to anyone. Mike will find out everything even though he's off the case. Let him tell you Stevie, keep it that way."

"Got it big brother, that's great news."

"Yep, it is. Just wanted to let you know. I gotta run, we're catching a movie."

"Sure thing Peter, bye."

His phone then rings again and the medical office comes on with a recorded message about how his blood tests are in the morning at nine o'clock and reminding him again that he should eat nothing for twelve hours prior. Juice and coffee are okay in the morning. What a personal touch.

Steve reads until he switches to watching the local news at five and the national news at five thirty. He feels tired again but is nearing the end of his Stephen King novel and he wants to see it through. Lori likes Stephen King too, and they often talk about the books each of them are reading. As he finishes the book, he has the urge to call her and tell her she should read it, then thinks better of it. They'll talk soon enough. Then he laughs to himself, trying to remember the last time Barry picked up a book. Probably years ago, for the securities examinations. To each his own. He eats the left-over pizza slices which aren't great reheated and a salad he made which is soggy, all in less than twenty minutes.

Steve waits until seven thirty then calls Candace. He has decided to totally leave this in her hands. "Hi Candace. How are you doing?"

"I'm fine Steven dear but I am so embarrassed, I was going to call you tonight because I forgot to tell you something." She sounds serious, no Doris Day happy lilt in her voice.

"Oh, what's that?" Did she forget to say she's dating someone else? She's been exposed to Covid? She was at a lepper colony recently? Stop it!

"My first cousin Kirsten, it's her daughter's bat mitzvah Saturday and the party's Saturday night at some restaurant in Wauneda, is it?"

"You mean Wauconda?" Steve answers.

"Yes, that's it, Wauconda." The titter follows. "I'm such a dunce. I should have told you Saturday before you left. We talked about so many things, and this was so obvious and, well, stupid me, I forgot. I talked to Linda, and she reminded me."

Steve doesn't know what to think. He reasons that it's an honest mistake but then again why did she take so long to let him know? She must have realized it the next day. All this is running through his mind but all he can manage is, "Oh, well okay then. No harm done. I was going to ask you what you were up to, but we can make it another time if that's okay with you."

He sounded hurt and she sensed it immediately. "Of course we'll make it another time. I'd say let's meet Sunday for brunch, but I know you golf."

"It's fine, really. We can make it the following week if you're open and, in the meantime, think of what you might like to do."

"Absolutely I will. How does your week look, doing anything special?"

"Not really. I've got blood tests tomorrow morning and a physical on Friday. I've been tired a lot lately, I think I mentioned it, and I want to see what's up."

"I would hope it's just age," she replies. "I know with tennis now; I sometimes struggle to get through a couple of sets let alone a match. And I'm finding it's hard to play two days in a row. I get tired and my shoulder hurts."

"I believe you have to get things checked out; you can't be overcautious."

She agrees with that. They went on and talked for another hour. She had, of course, heard about Stephanie, who was fine today as if nothing happened, and they talked about family issues, mostly hers. They agreed to talk Thursday night but if for some reason he knew the results of his tests sooner he should call her. He deeply appreciated that and told her so. She wished him good luck with the tests.

And so, Steve was left with a short-term disappointment but a long-term positive feeling. He settles in to watch the movie *Napoleon* on cable because when it was first out in theaters no one wanted to see it with him. After watching it, even though he thought Joaquin Phoenix was a great actor, he figured out why.

At nine-forty-five Lori calls. "Hi Daddy, just wanted to wish you luck tomorrow. Hopefully they'll figure out what's going on with you and hopefully again it's nothing serious."

"Thanks Lori, I sure hope everything's okay."

"It will be, and, by the way, Candace feels terrible about the weekend but please don't hold it against her, she really honestly just forgot."

"Jesus Lori, I just talked to her like two hours ago and you know what we talked about already?"

"Dad, she's my best friend's mother so naturally I know."

Steve can only shake his head. "I guess. Well, see you Wednesday. Village Green ballfield, right?" he asks.

"Yes, all the semifinals and final games are there now. And I don't know what you said to Noel in the car yesterday, but he told me he's not upset anymore about striking out that last time. He said he's 'past that.' Says he's 'moving on.' That sounds like something you would say to him or my gosh, that's something a forty or fifty-year old person would say."

"Or even a seventy-five-year-old, but I really didn't put it quite that way."

"It's okay Dad, it's good advice."

Steve gets ready for bed. Jeez, he thinks. Relationships are complicated. And exhausting. How do people do it over and over again?

CHAPTER TWENTY-TWO

Steve gets up, takes his various medications for blood pressure, cholesterol, type two diabetes and an overactive bladder, plus a pill for mild anxiety, and downs them with orange juice and coffee. Then he adds at least four vitamins. He dresses and checks the list by the garage door. Yep, he's got everything. He pulls out of the cul-de-sac onto Remini Drive down to Dundee and drives East to Pfingsten and South to the medical center near the infamous Westbrook Hospital.

He parks and goes into the huge, mostly glass with some brick added, building and finds the registration desk. He's been here many times. The lady at registration tells him that in addition to the blood tests and urinalysis his doctor has added an EKG because of his call to shorten the appointment. That will come after the blood tests and urinalysis.

He waits and is called within ten minutes by a pretty Black nurse who gives him the blood tests and a bottle to pee in directing him to a bathroom where he will leave a sample in a little box on the wall with a small door. Steve actually starts laughing in the bathroom. He usually has to urinate at the drop of a hat and three times at night and now, of course, nothing happens for about five minutes when suddenly it does.

He asks the same nurse when the test results will be ready, and she says to call Thursday. She then directs him down a long hall where another young nurse with a foreign accent asks him to lay down and take off his shirt. She then attaches electrodes to his chest and gives him the EKG exam. Steve always wonders about this test because it takes longer to put on and take off the electrodes than the test itself. Modern medicine.

After he finishes up, he realizes he is very, very hungry. It's almost ten-thirty and he has to go into Buffalo Grove to a baseball card shop because his grandson Randy has a birthday coming up and he collects baseball cards. He does know there's a Walker Brothers pancake and breakfast restaurant not too far from there. He punches the name and town (he tries Buffalo Grove first, then realizes it's in Arlington Heights) into his car's navigation system and it turns out he's less than two miles from there.

Steve settles into a booth and orders eggs benedict and fruit. His phone rings, Lori. "How did it go Daddy?"

"Oh fine, the doctor added an EKG. I'm at Walker Brothers on Dundee downing breakfast."

"By yourself?"

Steve sighs. "Yeah. I was hungry cause I had to fast so I couldn't call anyone at the last minute. Aren't you working today?"

"There's a Professional Development Day at my school today and since I'm a sub I don't have to go."

"Oh, well good for you."

"It's not good for me. As a sub if I don't work, I don't get paid."

"Oh, I'm sorry."

"Not your fault Dad, not to worry. Listen, I wanted to buy

you dinner tonight. I feel bad about Sunday. I was thinking that new deli on Waukegan just South of Lake Cook, Ernie's I think it's called."

"Aww, Lori, you don't have to do that. Like you said, not your fault."

"I know but I want to. Noel is eating at his friend Taren's house then sleeping overnight. Come on, it'll be fun. You can eat deli food once in a while, can't you?"

"Yeah, I spose' so. I've been watching my salt. Would I get you?

"Sure, I'm on the way, if you don't mind me sitting in your car."

"Funny lady. What time?"

"How's six-fifteen, I know you watch the national news at five-thirty."

"Am I that predictable?"

"Yes Dad, you are."

"Okay honey, my food just arrived so I'll see you later."

"Bye now, see ya' later."

Steve was angry with himself. She shouldn't be taking him out. Sure, she was ordering pizzas for everyone Sunday, but she was going to use coupons from Domino's. So, I've got to tell whoever seats us there tonight to make sure I get the check.

He dug into breakfast and noticed his shoulder and arm start to tingle again but the pain doesn't last too long, just a few minutes. He goes into the restroom and now could pee like the proverbial racehorse, pays his bill and heads for the card shop.

It was around noon and the shop was slow. Steve recognizes the owner, a guy in his forties with a beard and the owner recognizes him too.

"Hey, the watch guy, how ya doing?"

Steve liked the man but couldn't remember his name. At least he recognized him. "Good my friend, good."

"Whatcha wearing today, anything special?" He smiled, showing a row of brown teeth.

Steve shows him his wrist. "I've got an IWC Portugieser Chronograph from the eighties."

"Very nice my friend, very nice. What brings you in?"

Steve tells him he's looking for a Shohei Ohtani rookie card from 2023. Al, the owner's name, said he did have one, a Topps, and they negotiated the price a bit. Al says he's getting in an autographed one in a few days and asks Steve if they could maybe do a swap for the watch and a bit of cash. Steve laughs at that and says his grandson will probably end up with not only the card but the watch as well. Al got a laugh out of that too.

Steve goes up to Lake Cook Road but decides not to go home just yet. He is out of things to read, nothing on the Kindle or laptop and he decides he wants the feel, the touch, of a good old-fashioned book. He goes to what he thought was a Barnes & Noble up in Deerfield off Waukegan Road. But it's gone. Idiot! He should have looked first. Damnit. He uses his phone, and the closest Barnes & Noble is now on Skokie Boulevard amidst outlet stores. He shakes his head and remembers when Kroch's and Borders stores were everywhere. Don't people read anymore? I am a relic, he thought.

As he enters the store there is a big display for *The Heaven and Earth Grocery Store,* a best seller he heard about on PBS. Possible, but let's walk around first. He looks through fiction, non-fiction, historical fiction, which he liked and everything in between. He finds a book on watches but it's more of a coffee table type book than something to read, although the pictures are beautiful. 'Art for the Wrist' the caption says.

There are also people of all ages sitting in chairs just reading. This was fascinating to him. Did they work? Were they off today? Even at the bank, he couldn't sit and work, including reading, for long periods of time. He had to move or somehow be in motion. Even at meetings. As the senior vice president of a bank, he was known for having meetings that didn't last very long. The bank president, Norm Frankel, used to tell him 'If you can't get something done at a meeting in fifteen or twenty minutes it's a waste of time.' Steve had the same philosophy. His dad was like that. His patients and his own staff called him 'Nervous Dave,' never sitting for very long.

After what was almost an hour, he goes back to the front of the store and buys the original book he had looked at. When he returns to the house, he goes into the living room and starts reading. He notices that one of the wood planks in the floor is loose and it probably has to be lifted up and glued back. He has the glue gun in the garage, but it would mean getting down on his knees and that couldn't happen. He couldn't do that anymore without great difficulty getting back up which meant he would have to call Barry. Thinking about it he decided better to ask Stu to help. He'd mention it on Wednesday night. He continues reading, getting up and down to do this and that until about four-thirty when the phone rings.

CHAPTER TWENTY-THREE

"ello?"

"It's Mike, Stevie boy, you home?"

I am. Just reading and puttering around. Going to meet Lori for dinner. What's up Mike, anything new on the case?"

"Turn on the ABC Channel Seven News when it's five. Chuck Goudie's doing an exclusive story."

"Really, what happened? Did they catch someone else? Sheila and Nathan confess or something?"

"You'll see. Just watch. I'll call you back after the story."

"Aww, Mike, don't do that to me, just…"

"Just watch Steve and the truth shall be revealed as they say." He hangs up.

At five Steve watches. Sure enough, after the lead stories about turmoil in Gaza and wildfires out west they cut to Chuck Goudie with his serious tone and perpetual tan.

"Ravi and Cheryl, we have a story that led to the arrest of a

Chicago Outfit capo for the murder of a North Suburban attorney and it's straight out of *Goodfellas.*

Two weeks ago, criminal defense attorney Jack Heller was gunned down by the garage of his home in the North suburb of Westfield and almost immediately afterwards the Westfield police charged Heller's ex-wife, Sheila, and the couple's son, Nathan, with his murder. Well now the tables have turned because today the Chicago and Westfield police in conjunction with an FBI probe arrested Danny Caruso, a mid-level Outfit figure of their Chinatown crew for the murder. Several days ago, at Lou Mitchell's Restaurant on the near West Side (the camera moves to a shot of Lou Mitchell's Restaurant, then back to Chuck). Caruso met with a former mob member, seventy-eight-year-old Sal DiMucci or 'Sal the Pal' as he's called. Sal has the expertise in Outfit circles of removing bodies that no one wants found.

As it happens, Sal was about to be indicted by the FBI and Department of Justice for two murders ten years ago in Chicago Heights but agreed to flip on Caruso by wearing an audio and video wire. Caruso was then caught on tape admitting that he hired one Johnny Rossi who police have been looking for since Heller's murder. Now they know where he is as I'll explain. The motive was apparently revenge. If you remember at that big RICO trial last year Danny's father Mike and Mike's brother David were co-defendants in the same trial. Mike got off while David got twenty years. That didn't sit well with Danny who is known to be sort of a hot head with a long arrest sheet for assault and battery and theft.

Well now it's on tape why the police and FBI didn't find Johnny Rossi as Caruso admitted hiring Rossi to murder Heller, then killing him in an argument after he did. Caruso even told DiMucci where to find Rossi's body, inside a truck in Cicero. This story continues to develop, and we'll keep up as the details unfold but it's really the stuff movies are made of."

"Thanks Chuck. An incredible turn of events and uniquely Chicago," Ravi replies.

Steve can't believe what he just saw and heard. And he was right, Sheila and Nathan were going to be cleared of the murder. The phone rings again. "Steve?"

"Yeah Mike."

"Whadya' think?"

"I told you guys she and Nathan didn't do it. "

"I know but most people thought that. The thing is Danny Caruso could have got away with the whole thing if DiMucci didn't wear that wire."

"Yeah, I guess he could have." Steve smiles and nods his head.

"Listen, I have to get going. See you tomorrow night."

"Good deal Mike and thanks for the call."

"Hey Peter," Steve says as he calls his brother.

"What's up Steve?"

"Mike just called me to have me watch a newscast on our five o'clock local news. They had a big story on the David Caruso confession, and they added how Heller's wife and son will probably be declared innocent with charges dropped."

"Wow, I wish I could have seen it. You didn't let on did you?"

"Of course not. Even when the case is closed, I never will. Hey, you know you can stream the story. Just go to WLS TV Chicago, I'm sure they're running it."

"Thanks, little brother, I will. You know, I've been thinking, we shouldn't be strangers, life is short."

"I've been thinking the same thing, Peter. It's probably on me."

"No, not at all. You've gone through some tough times lately. I should have reached out more."

"Well tomorrow's a new day."

"Right, we'll make the most of it," Peter replies.

"Okay, I gotta run. Lori wants to take me out to dinner."

"What, really?

"Yeah, long story, but let's stay in touch."

"You got it."

Steve watches the five thirty national news and slips into a pair of jeans and an old Illinois Alumni tee shirt, gathers his keys, wallet, glasses and phone and checks his list on the door to the garage as he sets the house alarm, all good. He sighs as he starts the car and opens the garage door.

Months ago, he had told Barry where the safe was in the house and gave him the combination, letting him know that everything he needed to know, his will and trust, all accounts, insurance, instructions if he died, all were all in the safe. After all, Barry was his oldest and his executor. But now he felt the need to let Lori know as well. Not to get back at Barry or anything close to that but Barry seemed to be so preoccupied lately and so flustered. He was very proud of his son, especially with what he did with Noel, but it couldn't hurt to let Lori have the same information - or could it? He would bring it up and see.

Lori is just closing the door to her house as Steve pulls up. She looks pretty in a blue jumper, and she recently had her hair done. From twenty feet away he'd swear she looked just like her mother.

"Hi Daddy." She pecked him on the cheek.

"Honey, I have to hand it to you, I don't know if it's Noel's baseball, your ex paying you on time or what, but you seem a lot less stressed lately," Steve says as he pulls away.

"I'm just feeling better, that's all. It's probably all those things plus I just joined this single parent's group I heard about through a couple of friends."

"That's great. Is it like to meet people to date or socialize?" he asks.

"Yes, both." I'm going to my first event on Saturday night at a restaurant in Rosemont. After all, I have to keep up with you Dad. You found someone and now it's my turn," she smiles at him.

"Hey, wait a second Lori, it's been a couple of dates. I mean…"

"Oh, I think there'll be lots more. You two seem to fit."

Steve shakes his head as they pull into Ernie's parking lot. "I don't know, I still don't know what a woman like that sees in me."

"Your self-confidence is amazing Dad, just amazing."

They enter the restaurant, and Steve asks for a booth and since they had booths for two people or four or corner booths Lori piped in "how about that corner booth there?"

Steve looks at her oddly, "for just us?"

"Weeell," she said, "we may be meeting Linda. She called and her kids are out of town, and she sounded lonely so I asked her if she wanted to meet us. Don't be mad Daddy, she's my best friend and she's been there for me so many times and she may not even come."

"Yeah, okay," he says. There goes the talk about the safe. A minute or so after they're sitting together in the booth Linda comes in wearing a red and white UMass long-sleeved hoodie followed by Candace in a black leather jacket with a purple turtleneck and slacks. Steve, who was drinking water without a straw, suddenly finds some going up his nose.

"Oh, hi Lori, hi Mr. K," Linda chirps. "Thanks so much for including us at the last minute."

Steve turns to Lori and if he was a superhero his laser vision would have burned right through her. Then he slides out of the booth to hug Linda and then Candace who was behind her.

"You didn't know a thing about this, did you?" Candace whispers in his ear.

"Not at all, but it's okay," Steve whispers back.

It was awkward at first but after Steve asks Linda about her college days at UMass the mood lightens. Linda could have been a comedian in another life and Candace added a story about when she and her husband visited Linda for Parents Day that was also very funny.

Linda then asks Steve what was new, and he mentions rejoining the Chamber of Commerce, the Men's Club and his plans to do some additional volunteer work. Everyone thought that was great and Lori says she is proud of him, that it's time for him to move on. Steve said nothing but nods, and everyone could see his eyes were almost tearing up.

The food is good, not like the old Chicago delis but close enough. Steve has a chopped liver sandwich on rye with creamy coleslaw. Everyone has either matzah ball or kreplach soup. He thought that should be his salt intake for the week. The Dr. Brown's black cherry soda doesn't help his type II diabetes either.

They talk about their kids and grandkids (where applicable), especially what they were doing, what was popular like Tik Tok and bullying and if it was harder to raise girls or boys (girls won). When it starts to get late Steve catches the attention of the waitress and takes the check. Lori, Linda and Candace all loudly protest, and Steve puts his hand out like a stop sign and calmly says they can leave the tip. He tells them what that should be and has a sly smile for a second when the three women now fight about that.

As they walk out, Candace grabs Steve's arm and they walk ahead of Lori and Linda. "I want you to know I had no part in this and I'm extremely sorry. Linda called me and asked if I wanted to have dinner and that *maybe* Lori would be at the restaurant. I am so, so sorry."

Steve pats her hand and then holds it. "I understand and I got the same line of bull. She tells me at the restaurant that Linda might join us, a minute before you both walk in. I don't know what they hoped to accomplish. It's like we're two doddering old people who need them for us to connect. I'm the one who's sorry, for Lori's behavior."

They stop by her car and she releases his arm as he does the same. She looks at him seriously, her brown eyes looking into his. "I feel bad, and I want you to know that assuming you were going to call me for the weekend, wherever you want to go, whatever you want to do, it's fine by me." She presses her lips together, emphasizing how serious she is.

He laughs for a second. "I appreciate that and of course I was going to call you, actually tonight when we got home, before all this. And you don't have to agree on anything or everything, we'll talk and figure it out."

"You are a special guy, Steven Kaufman. We'll talk soon." She leans in and kisses him.

"Ditto Candace Miller."

Linda comes up behind them smiling. "Bye Mr. K. See you soon."

He looks at her with a scolding face. "Goodbye Linda. Behave yourself." She titters, just like her mom.

Lori is waiting by Steve's car, rocking back and forth on her heels because she knows what's coming. "You want me to walk home Daddy?" She gives a little laugh.

That scolding face is now directed to her. "Just get in," he replies.

He's ready to explode but holds back or tries to. "Lori, what were you thinking? Why do you think that she and I need to be pushed together? We're doing fine, maybe too slow for your generation but just fine. Antics like this could drive us apart, have the opposite effect. Please, I love you but don't ever do that again."

"I'm sorry, we didn't really think it through, thought it would be fun to be spontaneous, especially after she cancelled for Saturday." She looks away, out the window.

"Well, you were obviously wrong, and it ended up being okay but was extremely uncomfortable. When you're my age spontaneous isn't always good."

There is silence the rest of the way home. Lori thanks him for dinner and says she'd see him tomorrow at Noel's playoff game. Steve reminds her that now she really owes him a dinner, but he's smiling at her.

When he gets home his back, arm, and shoulder are bothering him again. He grabs some Halo sugar free ice cream and eats it out of the carton to get rid of the chopped liver taste in his mouth. And again, he feels tired, very tired, which nixes a walk he was going to take. After changing and popping his nighttime pills he is out, forgetting to set his alarm.

CHAPTER TWENTY-FOUR

Steve woke up at about eight with a headache and a stiff neck. The stiff neck was understandable because he was laying halfway down the bed and without a pillow under him. An Aleve tablet would take care of his headache. He rolled over and sat up, thinking of the dream he just had. He was walking in a park, and it was Spring. It was in the city as there were tall buildings on one side of the park behind a line of trees. Guys were playing in a pickup baseball game, but not just any guys, all of them were friends of his. Jeff, Dennis, and Greg were there. They were yelling for him to come and play. Dennis yelling, "Steve, we need another outfielder!"

He started to move towards the field, but his brother Peter suddenly appears, blocking the way, telling him he can't go on the field yet. Steve asked why, but Peter just shook his head. It wasn't the Peter he just saw last week but Peter from when he was twenty-one.

Seldom do dreams make any sense unless you're Freud. But Steve gasped because, without a doubt, this one made perfect sense. All the players were dead, and Steve wanted to join them, but Peter said it wasn't his time yet. He sat on the side of the bed and covered his face with his hands, which were trembling. Not yet, not yet.

He had some breakfast and turned on the TV while finishing his coffee. The local news was on and suddenly holding a press conference was Steve Morris, Jack Heller's partner. He was stating how all charges against his clients, Sheila and Nathan Heller, have been dropped. "From the beginning of this case, the authorities at all levels, state, county and local, knew full well that my clients had been framed, but it took a wiretap with a full confession from a prior felon for their innocence to be apparent to everyone." Morris took no questions, and the regular news continued as Steve turned it off.

Steve was going to call Mike, but he'd wait until Mike finished his shift. He got dressed and decided to call Dottie Kraft, the director of a small nursing home where he used to volunteer with Becky. "Hey Dottie Kraft, Steve Kaufman. How you doing?"

"Well, I'll be, Steven Kaufman. What's it been, about a year? I haven't seen you since the funeral. I'm so sorry. We all loved Becky."

"Thanks Dottie. How are you?"

"Gettin' along Steve, honey, gettin' along." Dottie had the distinction of being the head administrator of a nursing facility, mostly Jewish, while being from Euless, Texas, near Fort Worth. But she had a nursing degree and a master's degree in healthcare from the University of Texas at Austin. She was a smart lady, accent and speech pattern notwithstanding.

"Dottie, you still taking in volunteers?" he asks, thinking that sounded stupid, like the volunteers were cats or something.

"Sure, babe. What did you have in mind? A few hours a month on Wednesdays like before? And oh, by the way, today is Wednesday. Why don't you come on down here and we can chat? Love to see you even if you don't volunteer."

"Sure, Wednesdays work. And guess what? I have to stop by a car dealership right near you. You be around in an hour or so?"

"Where am I gonna go Steve, honey? You know where we are. The staff and I are just fixin' to put up some Fourth of July decorations with the help of our wonderful residents."

Steve laughs. It's like going back in time, a happier time. "You got it. See you soon."

After checking with the Lincoln dealership that his appointment to look at a rattle under the dashboard is still on, he goes outside to bring in the Tribune and sees the Heller story splashed all over the front page with pictures of Jack, Danny Caruso, Sal DiMucci, Sheila and Nathan prominently displayed. Certainly, the biggest crime in Westfield in easily ten years since an unhinged Korean guy blew away his wife and twelve-year-old son.

Steve takes the Edens Expressway South to Touhy in Lincolnwood and goes North to the dealership, pulling the car up to a service bay. They open the door, and Steve explains to the service manager, Carlos, again what the problem is and almost curses when he says to Carlos if he was just a little younger, he could bend down and take a flashlight and try to fix it himself. Carlos laughs, says it won't be long, and directs him to the customer lounge. There is a text message from Stu that he didn't catch because his phone ringer was off. He wanted to know if pizza from Pizzano's for tonight was okay. Steve just said, "Yep." Something Dottie would say as he smiles.

He starts to read an article in an old Car and Driver magazine when Carlos comes in and says they fixed the issue. Loose wires and connector switch. There was a seventy-five-dollar labor charge, which he paid with the gum chewing twenty-year-old cashier. Then he drives away to the nursing home about a half mile away.

Dottie Kraft greets him with open arms and a long hug, with her ending in tears when she brings up Becky again. Then she gives him a tour of the facility, which he fondly remembers, and introduces him to the staff, a few of whom he also remembers. He sees a few residents working on the decorations but doesn't recognize anyone. After about an hour, he says he'll be back next Wednesday at ten and says his goodbyes to Dottie and the staff. He feels tired and hungry, the hunger part satisfied by stopping at Portillo's on Skokie Boulevard before hitting the highway to go back North. He has a jumbo hot dog with all the trimmings but justifies it by ordering a side salad instead of fries.

Listening to Darius Rucker on the way home, he decides to try walking again and see if he has any pain or becomes tired. When he arrives home, he changes into his new HOKA running shoes and sets out for Lake Cook Road, again going down Remini Drive. He makes it there but then decides to go back. He has no pain and is not winded, but decides not to press his luck by continuing to run.

He makes it home and sees that Mike had called on his phone, which again was somehow on a silent ringer. Mike didn't leave a message, though. Steve calls back, and the call goes right into voice mail. Steve left him one, saying he thought Mike was calling about the Steve Morris press conference. It was now about three-fifteen and as he takes off his clothes to shower, he does feel tired again so he decides to take a nap, setting his clock radio *and* phone alarm for four.

Both alarms go off at four and he dresses and searches in the garage to find his little padded bench seat that fits over the hard metal bleacher seats. Michelle had gotten it for him for something, maybe Father's Day.

Then he panics. His wallet wasn't on his chest of drawers in the bedroom. He searches the kitchen, then the entire house. No luck. His face feels flush, and his heart is racing. Think Steve! You had it at Portillo's to pay. Could you have left it there? He checks the car and there it is, wedged between the door and the front seat. He heaves a sigh of relief and makes sure he has everything else on his door checklist.

Steve always sits in the front bleacher row at the games, putting the padded portable seat under and behind him so the next seat up isn't jutting into his back. There used to be a time when he was a father at games that he'd sit near the top of the bleachers to get a view of the entire field but these days with nothing to hold on to on his way up or down the seats and shitty balance, sitting up higher no longer worked. Now he was a lot closer, but the fence was in front of him. As his grandma Bess used to say, *it is what it is.*

Lori and Noel show up and she sits next to him, chatting away about the Heller case and asking if Heller was part of the Wednesday night group which Steve has told her at least ten times that he used to be but that his travel plans got in the way. She then apologizes again for last night, and he just nods.

Noel had gone from batting ninth to third and there was a runner on first when it was his first time batting. The pitcher throws wide, then low, then a pitch that Noel hits to center which the center fielder makes a play on but muffs it, the ball rolling to the outfield fence. Noel ends up on second and a run scores. Lori is screaming and Steve is cheering as well, although not quite with the same enthusiasm.

The Yankees maintained a one run lead for the next few innings until the Orioles, the opposing team, have runners on first and second with two outs. Noel was in right field, but not too deep, with runners on base. The batter fouls off two pitches, then hits a fly ball to right field. Noel is under it, and it lands on the edge of his glove and he bobbles the ball with everyone in attendance holding their breath. It was in then out of his glove but his other hand was there to secure it between his hand and glove. Out number three. The Yankees fans cheer and Lori has her arm around Steve. But her father didn't see it. His vision starts to blur, and he can feel himself falling forward, although he holds out his arms in front of him.

Steve awoke in a hospital room with many people around him. He opens his eyes and hears someone say, "he's awake" and others agree.

"What, where am I?"

"You're in the hospital Daddy, cardiac unit. You had a heart procedure, a coronary angioplasty with a stent. You had a heart attack at the little league game," Lori practically yells to him.

Steve scoots up a bit in his bed. He notices the tubes in his arms and up his nose and he looks around the room. He sees Lori, Barry, Michelle, Noel, Stephanie, Paul and Randy, the latter in his baseball uniform as if coming from a game, and Candace, smiling at him.

"You're gonna be fine Dad. Everything went smoothly. Your doctor's appointment just got pushed up, that's all," Barry says and everyone laughs. "You'll be out of here in a couple of days." He hands Steve a cup of water with a straw, and Steve takes several gulps.

"By the way Daddy, Uncle Peter is flying in right now to see you," Lori says.

Steve nods slightly, again looks around the room and suddenly, he bursts out laughing. He closes his eyes and continues to laugh. People are turning to each other.

"Daddy, we're glad to see you're in good spirits, but what's so funny?" Lori asks. Barry and everyone else are nodding, seeking an answer.

Steve looks at all of them. "I wanted to get the family together, but this is ridiculous," he says, as they all start to laugh. He then closes his eyes. He is on a ballfield in a large park somewhere near the lake and appears to be playing center field. A sharp single is hit towards him, and he picks it up on the bounce and throws to Jeff, the shortstop, who is covering second.

THE END

The Steve Kaufman Series
Book 1: August of 68'
Book 2: The Parallel Line
Book 3: Ready Positions

West Ridge Publishing Co.

Elliot Lei is a real estate executive with two prior nonfiction books. This is his third work of fiction. He lives in suburban Chicago.

You can connect with Elliet Lei below:
My email is: elliotlei063@gmail.com.
My X (formerly Twitter) account is: Elliotlei7

Acknowledgements:

I want to thank certain people who have been there for me throughout this trilogy and others with information and sources for this third book in particular:

Joe, Roxanne, Mark, Vance and Slater

E.L.